Hades

Velia Osiris

Contents

Prologue

P rologue

"Brother, listen to me."

The dark-haired man slowly swiveled around, his midnight-blue gaze empty. His reply was constrained by years of unending turmoil.

"What?"

His brother let out a long breath, his voice heavy. "Do not look at me like that. We are as upset by this turn of events as you are."

Disbelief flashed through the dark-haired man's eyes. "How can you say that? How can you look me in the eye and say that?"

"How were we to know?" The other's wizened features furrowed in frustration. "You did not show any indication you had feelings to be hurt. Even now, after everything that has happened, you have barely revealed your true thoughts. It is a rather frustrating quirk of yours."

"Forgive me then. I did not realise it was all my fault."

"Come now, Hades. We do not deserve your anger. We have acknowledged that this is not completely your fault. What more do you want?"

"You know what I want, Zeus." Hades turned away so his brother didn't see the pain flashing through his eyes. "It is more than a worthless acknowledgment."

Zeus' shoulders dropped, as if those six words bore a burden heavier than the world on his shoulders.

"And you know we cannot do anything about that, Hades. She is gone. To force her to return after she..." He shakes his head. "It is too unkind."

"Yes, I am well aware of that fact." Hades' voice clouded with anger. He shoved his hands into the pockets of his coat to prevent himself from doing something he would later regret. Blackened clouds started to roil around the two, boiling as violently as the fury seething through the dark god's veins. "I unfortunately had the luck to witness her escape, to watch as her eyes filled with unfiltered hatred the moment she saw me walk through the door. It is not a moment I will ever forget."

Zeus paused, his eyes flickering up and down his brother's hunched form. Understanding dawned on him; it was almost like he was seeing him for the first time. Moments passed. When he finally spoke, it was with slow, calculated precision, like one does when they're talking to a snarling beast. "We may never be able to understand your pain brother, I realise this now. But we do hope we can alleviate it somewhat."

"How?"

"We have a proposition."

"Yes, because your propositions end so well." Hades' voice dripped with venomous sarcasm.

Zeus gave him a look. "Come now, Hades. You know we never intended for it to end the way it did. The new proposition is not without consideration to that. If it bodes any reassurance to you, it is not one constructed by myself or any of the other twelve."

All muscle activity seized in Hades. His head slowly rose. "The Fates?"

"Yes." Zeus affirmed. "The Fates. They have a new prophecy, and it is for you."

Hades twisted to face his brother. Zeus was shocked into silence by the dangerous look darkening his features. A low rumble echoed around them.

"I trust the Moirai's propositions even less than yours." Hades spat.

"Hades—"

"No." Hades snapped. "They are the reason I am in this situation. They planted the seed of doubt in her mind. They are the last creatures in the universe that I would trust to prophecise the outcome of my future."

"You do not trust anybody Hades." Zeus replied sharply. His tone lost its hard edge when the clouds surrounding them began to rumble menacingly, growing thicker and darker than tar. "You know better than anybody that you cannot ignore their prophecies. The future they have seen will happen, whether you accept it or not."

Hades' jaw clenched. His words came out clipped. "What makes you think this prophecy will benefit me more than their last?"

"You and I both know that you cannot rule alone, and we don't want you suffering more pain than you already have." Zeus said. Hades scoffed disbelievingly. "We don't, brother. Already you are forgetting your duties; we can all see that. You and I both know that you will fade if you continue like this, and we cannot stand seeing you so despairing and lonely. Not even the King of the Dead deserves that."

Hades paused, studying the determination his younger brother was trying to prevent from filtering into his expression. "You are not going to relent until I listen, are you?"

Zeus smiled. "Of course not."

"Fine." Hades sighed, sounding tired. "What is their prophecy?"

"They have prophecised that you will find a queen. A mortal, this time. Perhaps the presence of a human soul will allow for more compassion and understanding—"

"Zeus." Hades cut him off, frustration lacing his expression. "I want their exact words. Not yours. I trust your word even less than theirs."

Zeus finally failed in keeping his own anger in check. A jagged bolt of lightning cuts through the black sky, tearing a gaping hole in the bubbling black clouds. But, all too aware of the boundless limits of his older brother's obstinacy, he grudgingly subdued his frustration and submitted to his brother's barked request.

"Hair of autumn, eyes of green, she is a treasure the world has not yet seen. For four months and not one day longer, your heart of ice this mortal must try conquer. Upon the 120th day, should she decide to stay, this hardened resilience to love will melt away."

Hades did not move a single muscle, for several long minutes; a reaction that would have terrified any other person — or divinity — to their very core. Finally, he met Zeus' gaze, his expression harder to crack than a wall of ice. "You are telling me that they have destined a mortal to try and find it in herself to love the God of the Dead?"

"Yes."

"Even a goddess could not bring herself to." Hades replied, his voice tinted with incredulity. "What makes any of you think a mortal will?"

Zeus smiled benignly at his brother. "Mortals can be surprisingly compassionate, Hades. You have only seen them when they are dead or in their Elysium. When they are alive they are quite different."

"You are still asking me to expect them to do exactly what she did." Hades closed off again, his midnight-blue eyes blank. "I will not put another through what she did, or watch them suffer a life they do not want because of me. I may be a god, but I am not immune to pain."

"And I will not watch you let yourself fade away because of what happened. We may not have had the best relationship in the past, but we are still family Hades." Zeus spoke sternly. "Which means I will not stand idly by and let you brush this prophecy off as folly. I will do what is necessary to ensure you do not fade into nihility."

Hades' eyebrow shot up. "Are you really blackmailing me, brother?"

The air around Zeus started to crackle with power as his wizened face grew serious. "Yes I am, Hades. But I am doing it for your own good."

Hades pressed his lips into a thin line. "Very well. I will not ignore the prophecy."

Zeus doesn't stop the relief from showing on his wise features. He placed a reassuring hand on his brother's shoulder. "Thank you, Hades."

"I will not ignore the prophecy," Hades continued, holding his finger up with a frosty glare before Zeus could interrupt him a second time. Though he had the more youthful appearance of the two, he was still the oldest, and could beat his younger brother into quiet submission with a single, hard look. "On one condition."

"What is it?"

"That she choose this voluntarily." Hades said. Understanding lit up the other god's face. "She must not be forced into any of this, nor know anything about the prophecy except from my own lips. If, for some reason, she finds it in herself to... care for me, without being forced or coerced by any deity, then I will accept that the prophecy has the potential to come true."

"Of course." Zeus nodded. "If she falls for you without the force of a god acting upon her, and she willingly chooses to, then she will stay in the Underworld and help you rule. If your condition is broken however, then she must return to her former life, and all memory of our existence will be wiped from her memory."

"Very well." Hades inclined his head, turning on his heel to disappear into the night. Zeus caught his shoulder before he had the chance to do so, giving the other god a firm look.

"It will work out this time, Hades. You just need to find the right girl."

Hades shrugged his hand off, his expression darkening. He vanished from sight, his words fading as he did. "I hope, for the sake of both you and the mortal, that you are right."

Chapter One

<hr>

C hapter One

I've never been afraid of death.

It's always surrounded me with its dark embrace, hovering above me like my own personal cloud of doom and stealing away those who got too close to me. It took my parents when I was ten, killing them in a car crash that almost took my life too. Six months later, it took the most important person in the world to me, through the most horribly contorted way possible. And only eighteen months ago, it took one of my best friends, donning the guise of cancer. Death was a cunning, twisted snake, and for some reason seemed morbidly obsessed with my life.

So, I wasn't unfamiliar with the heart wrenching, gut twisting pain that death delighted in handing out like candy. Despite that though, I wasn't afraid of my time: the time when death finally decided to stop knocking down the people I loved and take me instead. It sounds bizarre, I know, but I liked to convince myself that I needed to face my fears and not let them conquer me into blind submission. Being the obsessive person I am, I even took it one step further and often allowed myself to daydream about life after death, refusing to believe that we just stopped existing after our bodies gave up. We all had to go somewhere after we died, whether it be heaven, or hell, or purgatory. I refused to believe that death was the final, ultimate full stop to the end of our stories. Instead, I convinced myself that no matter what happened, no matter how or when I died, in this Heaven-esque world I would be happy. I would be happy, I would be with the person I loved, and the pain of life finally wouldn't be able to get to me. I would be free.

Little did I know, those daydreams would become a reality much quicker than I ever expected them to.

— — —

"Evie!"

I bob my head in time to my music, crossing my ankles and tapping my toes as I stare at the book in front of me. As determinedly as I stare at it though, the words on the page don't diffuse into my brain as easily as the words streaming into my ears do. Before I know it I'm humming along to the music, the page as good as blank to me.

Who would've guessed that reading a book for university wasn't as easy as reading a book for leisure? I guess the pleasure really is taken out of it when your whole university career depends on you reading that book.

"Hey! Autumn!"

My eyes snap up at the sound of my last name. I whip my head from side to side, my gaze already narrowed to scold the person who yelled out, and quickly spot the culprits striding through the row of trees behind me, grinning from ear to ear.

"Oh that's typical, now you hear me."

"It's hard not to when you bellow like that." I retort. "Seriously, do you think you could've yelled any louder? I don't think America heard you."

The one on the right snorts. "Do you really want to encourage him? You do know Spencer, right?"

"Is that a challenge I hear, Olly?" Spencer smirks, cheekiness twinkling in his blue eyes. I don't miss the gut-punch he aims at the dirty-blonde standing next to him.

"You hear everything as a challenge, Spencer."

I shake my head with a smile, pulling my headphones off my ears and letting them rest on my collarbone. "What are you doing here, boys? Don't you have a lecture, like right at this very moment?"

Spencer shrugs his broad shoulders, plopping himself down on the grass next to me. "Not anymore. For some reason, the lecturer seemed more than happy to oblige when we suggested they cancel today's lecture."

"Suggested or coerced?"

"What's the difference?" Olly snaps a twig off the tree behind me and hurls it into the lake glittering in front of us. "Either way, she was extremely receptive to our proposition."

"You two are despicable." I inform, my nose wrinkling in disgust. "Just because the lecturer is young doesn't mean you can flirt with them. Have you seen yourselves? You probably gave the poor thing a heart attack."

"What's wrong with that?" Spencer grins, gesturing to himself. "How can one not flirt with others when they have been blessed with a body as gorgeous as mine?"

"Could you be any more narcissistic?" I laugh. He, unfortunately, wasn't wrong, though. Everything about my best friend was perfect, from his golden, sunkissed and artfully ruffled-up hair, to his shining cerulean blue eyes, to his lean athletic stature, and he knew it. Oh boy, did he know it.

Even though he was probably the most genuine person in the world — the kind of person who would literally stop what he was doing to help an old lady cross the street — he was also the biggest player that I knew, and spent the majority of his time getting drunk at parties and wasting his education away. I'd say something to him about it, but all the times I've tried in the past he's just ended up laughing in my face and walking away. I'm pretty sure it just floats in one ear and keeps going out the other.

Like all other sensible and logical advice.

"Oh please, Spencer. Have you seen these guns?" Olly flexes his biceps. "You're kidding yourself if you think you're the hot one."

I roll my eyes. Olly was hardly any better than Spencer. He was the Tweedledum to Spencer's Tweedledee; sure, he was significantly taller than Spencer, his hair was more on the brunette side of blonde, and he clearly went to the gym more, but he was just as exuberant as Spencer was when it came to living life. If you ever had to describe a stereotypical jock, Olly was your guy, but he had a heart of gold, despite the way he went about it. I was always slightly reassured by the fact that whatever mischief Spencer was causing, Olly wasn't that far behind. Hell, Olly was probably the mastermind behind said mischief, but he always knew when to reel my best friend back in. It's almost like he'd been born to simultaneously cause mischief and worm his way out of reaping the consequences for said mischief-causing.

"I take it back. You're both narcissists."

"You say that like it's a bad thing." Spencer replies haughtily. He latches his hands behind his head and lies back in the grass, closing his eyes. "But I know for a fact that there are many, many people in the world who would disagree."

"People?"

"People." Spencer shrugs casually. "I'm not picky. That's far too much effort."

I smack him with my book and repeat my earlier statement. "You are despicable."

"Yet you love me." Spencer teases in a sing-song voice. I smack him again. He catches my book and rips it out of my grip. "What are you reading?"

"Probably yet another nerd book in Latin." Olly teases, throwing another stone into the lake.

"Oh please. Don't act like you're not fluent in Latin, Oliver." I snort. I snatch my book back out of Spencer's hands. "It's Herodotus' The Histories."

"So, a nerd book." Spencer smirks. I narrow my eyes at him.

"It's for my Greek History class. I thought I'd read a little bit of it before the lecture."

"You're such a nerd, Evie." Olly scoffs. "When is the lecture?"

"3pm."

"In four hours?" Spencer sits up just so I can see the look of disbelief on his face. "E, tell me you're not going to spend four hours reading that mumbo jumbo?"

I nod. His jaw drops.

"Why?"

I sniff, turning my nose up in the air haughtily. "Because I actually enjoy reading it? That's a thing, Spencer. People enjoy reading."

There's a skip of silence. Spencer stares at me. Olly turns around, his expression just as grave as Spencer's.

Oh boy. Here we go.

"It's not a 'thing', Evie," Spencer starts.

"It's an obsession, and it's unnerving." Olly continues without missing a beat.

"You already know all the stuff in that book," Spencer pipes up.

"You're just reading it for fun." Olly finishes, his nose wrinkling up in mock horror.

"Stop that. Stop that right now." I retort dryly. "What is your point?"

"That you need to get your nose out of mumbo jumbo like that every once in a while!" Spencer exclaims, stabbing my book with his finger. He flashes me a pearly-white smile when I give him an unconvinced look. "Because really Evie, you and I both know that you enjoy our company so much more than your silly obsession. You just need to start acting like it."

"I do act like it, Spence. I just prefer the company of my obsession over the company of your drunk selves, which you're letting out and about more and more every day. My obsession smells less." I glance at my watch and start shoving my book into my satchel. "I have to go."

"No you don't."

"Yes I do." I raise my eyebrows at him. "I just told you I had a lecture, Spencer."

"In four hours!"

Olly snickers, returning his attention to throwing stones into the lake. "You tell her, Spencer."

"That's not the only lecture I have today, you muppet." I snort. "Not all of us are able to skip every lecture and still get A grades, you know."

Spencer pulls a face at me. "What if I told you I was going to see the twins? Is that enough incentive to make the nerd in you skip your lecture?"

My eyes light up. Just like that, all thoughts of attending my lecture abandon my mind. "Are they back already? I thought they weren't meant to return until Friday."

"Flew in this afternoon." Spencer informs me, twirling the keys around his fingers. "I'm going to go pick them up now in preparation for their surprise party. Wanna join?"

"Hey!" Olly whines. "Where's my invitation?"

"I choked on it." Spencer deadpans. "You have that thing anyway."

"Maybe I don't want to do that thing."

"Trust me. You do." Spencer gives him a look. Olly harrumphs and plasters a wide-eyed pout on his face. "Oh, go shove that look up your arse, you know it doesn't work on me."

"What thing?" I ask curiously. Then I wave my hands in the air, jumping to my feet with a grin. "You know what, I don't care. I'm going to ignore the fact that they asked you, and not their own sister, to pick them up, and say yes."

Who am I kidding; Spencer was right. I knew the majority of the content taught in my lectures, so I wouldn't be missing out on anything anyway. That's what happens when you have an overly obsessive nature and a ridiculous amount of spare time; you find something interesting and suddenly you need to know everything and anything about it. I never knew whether to bless or curse my addictive nature.

I bid a hasty adieu to Olly and head to the university car park with Spencer, excitement fizzling in my veins. Despite the trip to the airport being relatively short, the drive seems to drag on in the unnaturally warm day. I didn't mind that at all though; we hardly got those in England, so one tended to enjoy it when the sun finally decided to smile down on us.

I wind down the window and lean my head against the car door, my hair flickering around my face in the breeze. It had almost been a month since I'd seen my older foster siblings. They were two of the best competitive archers in the world, and travelled everywhere their archery skills took them, sometimes spending months away at competitions. It didn't come as much of a surprise to me anymore though; they were crazy good at whatever they set their minds to. Just like everyone else in my foster family.

I blow out my cheeks, letting a long sigh flutter past my lips. Even though I loved my foster family as much as I'd loved my biological family, I couldn't help but sometimes feel like the bumbling rabbit stumbling around a group of elegant, insanely talented swans. Not a single member of my foster family was normal; every single one of them was internationally recognised for at least one skill or sport, and it was maddening. For the twins, Selene and Axel, it was archery; though my foster brother, Axel, was also widely recognised in our little township for being an incredibly talented musician. My foster mother, Minnie, on the other hand, was insanely smart, and could craft the most incredible items out of thin air. And then there was little, plain old me, whose biggest claim to fame was the number of Oreos I could fit into my mouth at one time. That's one of the reasons I obsessively pursued my knowledge of ancient civilisations; I felt like I needed to be good at something in order to keep up with the rest of them, and Oreo stuffing just didn't cut it.

"What are you thinking so hard about, E?" Spencer asks me, his warm tones cutting through my internal monologue. "It's giving you more ugly wrinkles, you know."

"That I'm a rabbit." I tell him truthfully. His face scrunches up in confusion.

"Not the weirdest thing I've heard from you, I have to say. But you're a beautiful rabbit, so that's okay." He chuckles, tapping his fingers on the steering wheel as he gazes around the airport carpark. He clicks his tongue in annoyance. "Do you want to head in and try to find them? I don't think I'll find a free park here."

"Yeah, sure." I unbuckle myself and jump out. I lean in the open window and wave my phone. "Text me your park?"

He nods and peels away from the sidewalk, belting out along to his music at the top of his lungs. I giggle at his antics and head into the airport, his voice echoing through the carpark behind me.

It doesn't take me long to find my foster siblings in the cool, air-conditioned building: I just follow the attention of literally every single person in the airport. The twins chat animatedly to each other as they stroll along, completely unaware of all the people ogling them. I'd grown up around their ethereal beauty, so I wasn't fazed by it anymore, but it was always a weird feeling seeing other people openly staring at them.

"Evie!" Selene cries as soon as she spots me, a bright beam spreading across her lips. "Long time no see!"

"Hey Selene!" I grin, waving at her. My grin falters slightly when I notice the spot to her right is unusually vacant. "Where's—"

Strong arms suddenly sneak around my middle, and I'm launched high into the air. I squeak in surprise, hastily grabbing hold of the person's shoulders as the world starts spinning.

"Axel! Put me down!"

A deep laugh reverberates through my body. I'm set down to the ground by a grinning green-eyed brunette. "Still as fat as ever, I see."

I scowl at him in pretense offence and cross my arms. "Still as big of a prat as ever, I see."

Axel's grin widens. He clutches at his chest like I've shot him. "Your words are deadlier than bullets, dear sister. You wound me greatly."

I stick my tongue out at him. "Keep up that sarcasm and I might just wound you greatly."

Rolling her eyes at our dramatics, Selene wraps her arm around my shoulders and starts steering us towards baggage claim. "Not that I love seeing you Evie, but where's Spencer? He was supposed to pick us up, and we were kind of going to surprise you."

"You were?" I raise my eyebrows at her. "Do you really need to question why that hasn't ended the way you planned?"

"No, not really." She sighs, scrunching up her nose. "He's completely useless, that one. I blame the extraordinary amounts of alcohol that he seems intent on consuming for his momentary lapses in any memory function."

I snicker and point at the baggage claim. "Go grab your bags before the useless one completely forgets about us. I'll bring a trolley over."

"Yes boss." Selene nods, chuckling as Axel mock salutes me.

"You know, one of these days, he's going to drink himself into a stupor and end up dead in a cave again. And between you and I? I am not looking forward to healing him of that endeavour." Axel mutters under his breath as they walk away, cringing when Selene elbows him hard. I give his retreating back an odd look, but don't question him on it. I've learnt that when he says things like that, it's not meant for my hearing. He's just terrible at waiting until I'm out of earshot.

Because the airport is so busy, it takes me several long minutes to navigate my way through the thick crowds to the trolley bay. As I'm about to grab the last luggage trolley in the bay, someone brushes past me, in such a hurry that they rip my feet out from underneath me and send me flying into someone else. A gasp is torn from me as I bounce off someone's back, landing hard on the ground. I groan, my backside throbbing painfully, and glare in the direction of the person's retreating back.

Asshole.

"Are you alright?" A warm, melodious low voice asks from behind me. I glance up to meet the magnetic midnight-blue gaze of a young man, who's watching me with a curious expression. My heart stops. I freeze, staring up at him with wide eyes.

"Um—yeah—uh—I'm fine—" I start to stutter, but before I can finish stammering, he's gone. I blink in bewilderment, staring at the spot the tall, dark stranger had inhabited mere seconds ago.

Well. That was weird.

"Evie!"

The sound of my name jolts me out of my confused reverie. Leaping to my feet, I dust my jeans off and grab the trolley, casting a glance over my shoulder one last time. Unbridled curiosity burns through my veins.

Who was that?

Shaking my head, I quickly locate the twins and head back over to them. We load all their luggage on the trolley, before striding out into the mild warmth of the setting evening.

It doesn't take us long to find Spencer's grape-purple car, haphazardly parked on an angle over two parks. Rolling my eyes at my friend's laziness, I pop the boot for the twins' bags and head round to the passenger's side. My hand pauses on the door when I hear his conversation.

"—damn it, it's too early!" Spencer spits. I blink in shock, taken aback by the venomous anger in his tone. "She's not ready!"

Ignoring the little voice in the back of my head telling me to respect his privacy, I lean closer, unable to repress my curiosity.

"You know that's not fair on her! Think about how it'll affect her!" He growls. "Don't get prissy with me man, I'll speak to you any way I want when it comes to Evie."

My eyes widen. My curiosity grows from a meek little cat into a raging lion. Who's he talking to? What's he talking to them about? And what does it have to do with me?

The person on the other end of the line talks for several long moments. Spencer sighs, not sounding pleased. "Fine. I guess I don't have any other option then, do I? But I hope you're ready to pick up the pieces from the mess—"

"Evie?" Selene speaks up loudly from behind me. I jump and whirl around, cursing inwardly at my sister's impeccable timing. She tilts her head to the side, her expression wavering between confusion and curiosity. "What's going on? Why are you just standing there?"

"I uh..." I falter, hoping to hear more of Spencer's conversation. He shuts down as soon as he hears my name, mumbling a short goodbye and shoving his phone in his pocket. My shoulders slump in disappointment. "Never mind."

Grudgingly, I slide into the car, ignoring the way Spencer stares at me.

"Hey Spencer!" Selene smiles, hopping into the backseat of the car. Axel joins her, folding his long legs up to fit himself in the small car. "Nice surprise seeing you here."

Spencer winces as he starts up the car. "Yeah, sorry about that. I just remembered that small detail."

"You really cannot be trusted with anything." My sister sighs in exasperation. She doesn't lose her smile, though; but that's Selene for you. She's far too kind for her own good, and has never been able to hold a grudge.

"That's common knowledge, Sel. Keep up with the programme." Spencer shrugs, pulling out of the car park. He raises his eyebrows at them in the rear-vision mirror. "How was the competition?"

I didn't miss the emphasis he placed on competition. I glance around at them all curiously. Am I missing something?

"Alright." Axel replies guardedly. "Pretty boring at times. It dragged on for a bit."

"It was good." Selene says firmly, giving Axel an unreadable look.

I turn back to the front and agitatedly tap my finger against the side of the car, pressing my lips into a thin line. After a few moments of uncomfortable silence, I look over at Spencer, injecting nonchalance into my tone. "Who were you talking to before? It sounded pretty intense."

His grip on the steering wheel tightens. His voice remains light and impassive. "Nobody important. Just a guy who's about to make a big mistake."

I smile at him reassuringly. "I'm sure it'll be fine."

"I hope so." He replies shortly, sharing a look with the twins in the mirror. Selene shakes her head once, almost imperceptibly. Spencer huffs, his eyebrows knitting into a hard line. The conversation is, once again, swallowed up by silence. I scowl at a passing tree.

Great. More secrecy. Just when I thought I had managed to stop letting that affect me after...

I swallow and keep my gaze fixed out the window, unable to restrain the irritation from filtering into my tone. "I didn't come to see you guys just so you could all hide things from me. You know how I feel about secrets."

"Sorry Evie." Selene apologises softly, but doesn't say anything further. The other two remain radio-silent.

I glare at my reflection and stare at the trees flashing by, the setting sun hooding their limbs in spindly shadows.

Sorry doesn't make it better. It never has. It's only ever made it worse.

Closing my eyes, I mentally throw up my walls again, refusing to let myself return to that dark place in my mind. Instead, I divert my mind to wandering over the events of the last day, running through them all like an old-school movie reel.

And through every scene, a pair of magnetic midnight blue eyes haunt me, watching me from the shadows of my memory. A singular question repeats in my mind like a stuck record, my curiosity rendering the record player broken.

Who are you?

Chapter Two

C hapter Two

"Well, would you look at that." A voice drawls the moment we walk through the front door. It's followed mere seconds later by the appearance of a familiar brunette woman, who's curled up on the couch, nursing a large glass of wine. "The prodigal children have returned!"

"Hello to you too, Minnie." I roll my eyes, throwing my bag at the couch. She grins, raising her wine glass up in the air in acknowledgment. I narrow my eyes at her. "Hang on. If they're the prodigal children, what does that make me?"

"A work in progress." She replies simply. "It's taken me almost nine years, but I think I'm finally getting somewhere."

"Hey!"

"Spencer, is this supposed to be the surprise party you had planned? Minnie and her bottle of wine?" Axel asks, raising an eyebrow as he surveys the room. "Because dude, your party sucks."

Spencer gasps loudly, staring at my foster brother like he'd just roasted a live puppy.

"You take that back, Axel! You take that back right now!" Then Spencer pauses, frowning slightly as he visibly processes Axel's sentence. "Wait, how do you know about the party?"

"I know everything." Axel replies coolly. "Just like I know you're about to have a drink of Minnie's wine without her noticing."

"What?" My foster mother whips around, just in time to see the bottle pausing in front of Spencer's lips. "Spencer! Put that bottle down before I gut you with a spear!"

"Told you. I know everything." Axel holds his hands up in the air. Selene snorts, shoving him and his bags upstairs.

"If you keep talking you're going to be the gutted one, Mr Oracle."

Spencer makes a noise of disgust. "Minnie, what the hell kind of wine is this? It's abhorrent."

Minnie's eyes narrow. Seconds later, a pillow is launched through the air at his head. Spencer somehow manages to both duck it and prevent the wine from spilling as he takes another sip.

"If it's that bad then go and buy your own."

"I don't buy my wine." Spencer scoffs. "What do you think I am, some kind of peasant?"

"Yes. That is exactly what you are."

He huffs, turning his nose up in mock offence. "I think you need to be fired as Evie's foster mother. You are an equally shocking person and a terrible influence on her."

"Spence, you are at least ten times worse." I pipe up, watching their exchange with incredible amusement. He swivels around with a smirk, pointing at me with the wine bottle.

"You know it baby."

Minnie clicks her tongue, glaring at the back of his blonde head. "Spencer, that's not something you should be proud of."

"Minnie, darling, it will always be something that I'm proud of." Spencer clicks his fingers at me, motioning me forward. "Come forth, Evelyn."

"You have to know that's not my name." I fold my arms over my chest and arch an eyebrow at him. "And why?"

"So you can finish this bottle of wine for me. I need an excuse to open another bottle. Another, better, bottle." He corrects himself. "This one is gross, and I have no intentions of going to the twins' surprise party full of gross wine. That's basically a felony."

Minnie pushes herself up to her feet, giving him a stern look as she passes him on her way to the kitchen. "Spencer, you better not be planning on getting drunk on my leather couch. While I don't condone typical student behaviour, I do condone typical student behaviour on my very expensive leather couch."

Spencer groans loudly. "Fine. We'll go and get drunk in Evie's room instead."

I blink. "Wait hang on, I don't—"

Before I can finish my protest, he drags me away, clattering as childishly as he can up the stairs to my room.

Kicking open my bedroom door, Spencer takes a big swig and throws himself down on my bed, splaying his long, gangly limbs out like a star. I gingerly follow, folding my arms over my chest as I watch him.

"Spencer, if you're going to get yourself drunk again, please do it on the floor. I am not cleaning my bed spread. Again."

Spencer grins, dutifully sliding off my bed. "That was a good night."

"For you it was." I mutter, falling back onto my bed with a loud and over-extended yawn. Spencer slaps my calf, ignoring my yelp of pain.

"Hey! You better not be yawning right now, Evelyn Autumn!"

"My name is not Evelyn. My name has never been Evelyn."

"That's irrelevant." He waves his hand, smacking me again. "Stop being tired and start being drinking."

"First of all, ow." I gripe, kicking his shoulder as hard as I can. "Second of all, 'start being drinking' does not make any sense. At all."

"Is there going to be a third of all?" Spencer asks me after a lapse of silence, leaning back just so I can see him raising an eyebrow at me. "Because you never say a first and second unless you're intending to berate me most vehemently on the 'third of all'."

I poke my tongue out at him childishly. "Yes. Third of all, what brought on this sudden urge to drink anyway?"

"So I can turn up to the twins' surprise party properly drunk. Duh."

"Spencer, you always turn up to parties drunk; you're basically the god of partying." I respond dryly. "But you never start this early, and you're never this angsty when you drink. So what's the real reason?"

Spencer shrugs. He investigates the neck of the bottle closely, very clearly avoiding my gaze. "I'm angry. I drink when I'm angry."

I shuffle around on my bed and lean on my elbows so I'm facing him head on.

"Why are you angry? Is it because of me? Wait no, it can't be because of me, I didn't do anything overly annoying today." I hum good-naturedly as I think, tapping my chin. "Does it maybe have anything to do with that conversation you were having in the car earlier?"

He frowns, taking a long swig. His answer contradicts his actions. "No. It's none of your business anyway, Evie."

"I'm your best friend Spencer. Of course it's my business." I soften my voice, trying not to let his biting tone get to me. "Stop lying and just tell me already. You know I don't like it when people lie to me."

He snorts bitterly. "That's ironic."

"What's ironic?" Now it's my turn to frown at him. I can't help but feel a little hurt by his words, even though I know he's already well on his way to being drunk. He shrugs. "Spencer, when is it going to get through that thick skull of yours that I hate secrets? You're the one who's had to pick up the pieces every other time a person has kept things from me; I thought our friendship meant more to you than that."

"Don't pull that emotional bullshit on me Evie, you know it doesn't work." Spencer retorts, his tone cutting. " I'm allowed to keep secrets from you if I know the truth will hurt you. It's called being a caring friend."

I glare at him. "Don't you know one thing about me? I can look after myself fine. I did before I knew you and I will after I know you. That's just an excuse, and you know it. Caring friend my ass."

Spencer laughs mockingly.

"I know a lot about you Evie, enough to safely call myself your caring best friend." He leans forward, staring me down with an intense gaze." But how well do you know me? What makes you think you can dismiss what I'm saying so easily?"

A chord strikes inside me. I stare at him, and am startled when I see how unusually devoid of emotion his eyes are. I thought I knew him — he had been my best friend since I was ten years old. Sure, I didn't know much about his family or his past, but that wasn't without the effort of trying. He had always been vague when we breached those topics, and changed the subject as quickly as he could. All that I really knew was that he was my closest friend: he was weird and funny and had a little bit of a drinking problem (okay, a big drinking problem), but I loved him nonetheless.

But I'd never seen this side of him, this bitter and twisted side. Chewing on the inside of my lip, I speak softly.

"What's going on, Spencer? Why are you attacking me? Are you trying to make me angry at you?"

He cocks an eyebrow at me. "Is it working?"

"Yes." I narrow my eyes. "Who the hell was on the other end of that phone conversation and what did they say that pissed you off this much?"

Spencer chugs down the rest of the bottle of wine and wipes his mouth with a flourish. He sways slightly on his feet as he throws himself upwards. "As I said Miss Autumn, it's none of your business. And honestly? I couldn't care less if that upsets you, because everybody lies about everything. You just need to buck up already and grow a thicker skin."

I raise myself up to my full height and glare daggers at him, unable to suppress the fury simmering in my veins any longer. "Spencer, I love you, but if you don't stop being an ass I'm not going to be able to restrain from punching you."

"I'm always an ass, E. Get over it." He sneers at me. My eyes bug out as I stare at him in disbelief. He points in my face, narrowly missing poking me in the eye. "Now, this ass is going to go and get wildly drunk at a party; a party that I'm officially redacting your invitation to, by the way. I don't want you to ruin it with your negativity."

My jaw drops. Spencer bows overdramatically and storms out, banging into the doorframe on his way out. My feet stay rooted to the spot. I faintly hear him say to someone "it's done," before the front door slams, and he's gone.

I blink back tears and let out a loud growl of anger, slamming my door shut in a fit of fury. After glaring at the door for several more seconds I throw myself down on my bed, muffling my screams of frustration with my pillow. I know that he was drunk and probably didn't realise what he was saying, but that still didn't take the bite off his words, or make what he said okay. I just couldn't understand why he suddenly decided to attack me. It didn't make any sense. All I did was ask if he was okay, and he acted like I'd skinned a cat in front of him. My curiosity was definitely justified too; he'd been fine all afternoon, up until he'd received that phone call.

That phone call. I scowl at my pillow. I don't know who was on the other end, but they had clearly discussed me at obvious length with my best friend, which, for some unknown reason, had turned him against me.

And for that, I hated them. In that moment, I hated them with every fibre of my being.

I turn to my side, staring blankly at the spot Spencer had inhabited not five minutes ago. I don't move for several minutes. In the midst of all my dogged attempts to process what happened, I shudder, my body unexpectedly hit by a tidal wave of exhaustion. All of sudden I'm drowning, and I struggle to keep my eyes open. My good conscience fights desperately to keep me awake; despite everything, I don't like the idea of Spencer going out in the state that he's in, particularly in the mood he's in.

But then my bitterness returns with a whole armada fuming about my best friend's caustic behaviour, and suddenly my good conscience's worries go up in a puff of smoke.

He'll be fine. He'll have the twins with him. Besides, he can obviously look after himself. He said it before; he doesn't want me or my negativity around. Why would I turn up when I'm obviously not wanted?

So, with the scowl firmly fastened on my face, I switch off my light and turn over into a restless sleep.

— — —

It feels like I barely get ten minutes of sleep before the veil of sleep surrounding me is ripped to shreds by the shrill ringing of my phone. Grumbling unintelligibly, I reluctantly roll over and peel my eyes open, grudgingly peering at my alarm clock. 2:47am. I groan loudly and glare at my phone. Who the hell is calling me at 3 in the morning?

The caller ID flashes at me obnoxiously. My glare deepens. Of course it's him.

"Spencer, what do you want?" I growl, answering the phone. "It's 3 in the morning and I really don't have the energy to talk to you right now."

"Evie?" I'm instantly awake when I realise the voice on the other end is not Spencer's. "This is Evie, right?"

"Yes, it is." I reply, sitting up in bed. "Who is this?"

"It's Leia. I'm a friend of your sister's." She says, struggling to make herself heard above the raucousness of the party. She yells at someone behind the phone. "Olly shut up! I'm on the phone!"

"Oh. Hey Leia." I sigh, rubbing my face in confusion. "Not that it's not good to talk to you or anything, but why are you calling me from Spencer's phone?"

"Spencer's drunk." She replies blankly, and I snort. No surprises there. "As in, so drunk he can't stand up. Can you come get him? We're all really worried about him, especially the twins."

I'm worried for all of two seconds before I remember what happened before Spencer's departure from my room. My sympathy withers up. "He can look after himself, Leia. He made it perfectly clear that he doesn't need or want me around him."

"Evie, please." Leia begs. "Whatever he said to you, he probably didn't mean it. He's the king of saying idiotic things when he's drunk. You can be angry and yell at him to your heart's content later, but right now I'm worried he's going to do something really stupid if you don't come help."

"He already did something stupid Leia." I deadpan. "Look, I appreciate you trying to look out for him, but he made it abundantly obvious that he doesn't want to see me tonight. And quite frankly, I don't want to see him."

"You know that's not true. How would you feel if he died or something terrible happened to him because you didn't come and get him? He needs to go home. And have a glass of water. And quite possibly have his entire body volume replaced with something that isn't alcohol."

"Why exactly can't you take him home? Or literally anybody else who is at the party with him? It's three a.m., Leia." I reiterate with as much emphasis as my exhausted mind can muster.

"I think you underestimate Spencer's power to get literally every single person at a party drunk, Evie." She replies dryly. "I've been drinking, just like everyone else. Otherwise I would take him home. Look, I know what the time is and I'm sorry, but could you please just come?"

I screw up my face in frustration before finally giving in with a groan, rubbing my face with my hand. Damn my good conscience. "He's lucky I like you, Leia."

She sighs in relief. "Thank you Evie. I'll make sure he doesn't do anything exceedingly stupid until you arrive."

"Yeah, good luck with that." I snort. Leia laughs breezily, hanging up after saying a hurried goodbye.

With a loud sigh, I reluctantly extricate myself from my warm bed, slipping on my old boots and my favourite hoodie over my ragged penguin-themed pyjamas. Once I've checked that my attire is at least semi-decent, I grab the keys to my foster mother's car and quietly slip out the door into the darkness.

Fortunately for me, Leia made sure to text me the directions while I was still dragging myself out of sleep's clutches, so it doesn't take too long to find the party. I pull into the first park I find and switch the car off, staring listlessly out at the mansion Spencer had somehow managed to hire out for the twins' welcome home party.The noise of the deafeningly loud music thumps through my car, reverberating through my body. I let out a long breath and hop out of the car, shoving the keys into my pocket. If I wasn't so frustrated and worried about Spencer, I'd probably be more self conscious about my hoodie-penguin pyjama combination, but I'd passed the point of caring. I just want to get this over and done with so I could go back home to my warm, comfy bed. I just about drool at the thought of it.

"Evie?" I turn to see a beautiful, slender blonde girl standing in the doorway of the mansion. She rushes down the steps to me, as graceful as a gazelle, a worried look plastered on her dainty features. "Oh, thank God you're here. Spencer is about ten seconds away from jumping off the roof."

"Hey Leia." I smile minutely, folding my arms tightly across my chest. "Where is he?"

"He's just in—"

"Evie!" Leia's cut off by a drunken shout. Found him. Spencer staggers up to us and throws his arm around Leia, grinning widely at me. "What're you doing here? I told you to stay away. I don't like your negativity, 'member?"

"Yeah, well, I'm not your biggest fan right now either, Spencer." I reply sourly.

He points at me, accidentally poking my face. Hard. "See that, that's the negativity I'm talking about. Begone, negativity!"

"Ow Spencer." I scowl at him, grabbing his arm. "Come on, we're going."

"What?" He rips his arm out of my grip and pouts. "Why? I want to stay here and get drunk." He drags the last word out, waving his bottle around in the air as if that one small action proves his point.

I roll my eyes. "I'm pretty sure you've already achieved that, Spence."

He hiccups and beams at me. "Really? Awesome!"

I groan and look at Leia, who's barely holding back a grin. She gives me the thumbs up. "Spencer, let's go."

"But I wanna stay." He whines, looking at Leia. "Lee, tell her. Tell her I need to stay. People need the King of Partying at the party."

"The King of Partying isn't going to do much if he can't stand up." Leia laughs, flipping her golden curls over her shoulder. "Just go, Spencer. I'll hold down the fort for you."

"Fine. But I swear to wine, if one person doesn't have a good time, I'm burying you in the ground." He grumbles, throwing his bottle at the ground as hard as he can. It breaks, sending razor-sharp glass shards scattering everywhere. I raise my eyebrows. Spencer completely ignores me, storming off in an obvious huff.

Alcohol sure makes him moody.

I glance back at Leia again. She shrugs with a smile. "Thanks Evie."

"Autumn come on!" Spencer yells over his shoulder as he starts to cross the road to my car. "The longer you stand there and gossip, the more time people have to realise you're at a party in your penguin freaking pyjamas!"

"Spencer—" Just as I start to yell at him for his shockingly loud and incredibly obtuse insult, I see something that stops the sentence short in my throat. A bolt of fear shoots through me like an arrow. "Look out!"

Spencer turns, just in time to see the truck plow straight into him.

Chapter Three

C hapter Three

Everything seems to happen both instantaneously and in slow motion all at the same time. The truck hits Spencer. The loudest bang I have ever heard in my life echoes all around us. Spencer drops like a stone. His body is snagged by the truck's bumper bar and dragged along the road for several metres, before he's sucked underneath the truck like a vacuum. I scream and run towards him. A hand grabs me and wrenches me back. The truck lets out a loud groan and speeds away, leaving a limp body in its wake. I suddenly lose the ability to breathe, or move, or function, gulping like a fish out of water as I stare blankly at Spencer. Leia, obviously deeming that I'm no longer in danger of being run over myself, relinquishes her grip on me and turns on her heel, screaming out words that are incoherent to me as she sprints back into the mansion. Time all but seems to stop. I tear my gaze away from Spencer and slowly look up.

And I meet a pair of magnetic, midnight blue eyes.

"You!" I gasp. A jolt of recognition freezes my limbs. "It's you!"

The man I'd met in the airport steps forward, watching me impassively. He looks around my age, no older than twenty-five. "Hello."

"Who are you? And what are you doing here?" I ask, finally managing to rip myself out of my petrified state enough to take a few steps forward. Spencer lies on the ground between us, scarily motionless.

The man tilts his head to the side, not unlike the way one does when they're observing a particularly interesting animal. His black trench coat flaps in the wind, revealing chinos and a shirt that are slightly different shades of the dark colour. "Don't you know?"

"Do I look psychic to you? Of course I don't know who you are!" I snap, throwing my hands up in the air. I stop myself, taking a deep breath. "Why am I talking to you? I shouldn't be talking to you, not when Spencer..."

Reality crashes down around me like a tidal wave. I stagger back, my heart leaping up into my throat. I stare up at the man in panic.

"Spencer. He... he got hit by a truck. I need to help Spencer. Why aren't you helping Spencer?!"

"Spencer is dead." The man says bluntly. "He cannot be helped."

"He's not dead!" I exclaim, near hysterics. "He can't be. He's Spencer."

The man doesn't respond, his gaze slowly lowering to the body lying between. I follow his gaze and finally, really look at Spencer.

And it hits me, right then, that the stranger's quietly spoken words might actually be true.

His body is twisted in such an unnatural position that I just know his spine is broken, along with what looks like half of the bones in his body. There's a deep dent concaving the side of his head in, and the blood that's already oozing from the wound streams down his cheek to meet up with the blood trickling out of the corner of his mouth. But what's most horrifying of all is his eyes. They're wide open, and blank as a slate. Unblinking.

My whole body revolts, and I struggle to keep myself from vomiting. Crashing to my knees, I frantically feel for a pulse, but there's nothing. No movement whatsoever. My chest tightens. Burning panic tears through my veins.

"Spencer! Wake up!"

"He is not going to wake up." A soft voice says from above me. I jump about a mile into the air. "Even if he did, why would you want him to wake up? From what I heard, he was not treating you very fairly."

"What the hell do you mean?" I demand. My gaze whips up in furious disbelief. "Of course I want him to wake up! He's my best friend!"

"Is that how best friends treat each other?" The man asks evenly. His midnight blue eyes glint in the dark." Like dirt? Filth? No care or respect at all?"

"He was drunk. He says stupid things when he's drunk. Everyone says stupid things when they're drunk." I snap my mouth shut and shake my head violently, shocked that I'm even indulging this lunatic in conversation. I lean down and frantically start giving Spencer CPR. "Why are you still here? Why aren't you trying to call for an ambulance? Spencer's dying, and I need someone to call a freaking ambulance while I try to keep him alive!"

"You have already failed at keeping him alive. He is dead." The man's voice is painfully matter-of-fact. "He has been dead for several minutes. Yelling at me will not change that. Neither will chest compressions."

"How can you say that?" I cry. "Please, just help me save him. Stop saying that and help me."

"Help you?" He says, sounding bemused. "How can I help you?"

"I told you how!" I start trembling, unable to restrain the panic attack rising up within me. "Call an ambulance! Or help me figure out exactly what's wrong! Just do something!"

The man sighs and kneels down opposite me, his coat rustling. The air between us is stiflingly silent as he studies Spencer, pressing down on me like a suffocating fog. Finally, he turns his gaze back to me. His blue eyes stare right through me as he speaks.

"He has a fractured skull. The impact has caused his brain to swell and bleed, and several of his facial bones have fractured. Three of his ribs have snapped, and the shards have pierced his heart. His spinal cord has been severed, and several of the bones in his lower body are broken. The impact of the truck alone has caused excessive internal haemorrhaging, and even if he were alive, his organs would not have sustained him for much longer. But all that is irrelevant. As I have said, he is dead."

His tone is so impassive and unfeeling that my stomach flips, turning on itself. I glance back down at Spencer, and realise for the first time that one of his eyes is no longer in its socket. This time, I can't keep the vomit down.

Once I've finished retching, I wipe my mouth with the back of my hand and falteringly look back at the man. Terror creeps into my tone. "Who are you?"

"I am known by many names." He straightens back up, towering over me like a dark statue. "But the name I commonly go by is Hades."

His calmly spoken words deliver a swift punch to my gut. Oh, you've got to be kidding me.

"No. No, this is going too far. I know some people are twisted in the head, but this is just sick." I laugh emptily, winding my arms around my stomach as I stand up. "How dumb do you think I am? You're not a god, and Spencer is not dead! This is all just some sick prank!"

He raises an eyebrow. "You are being pointedly oblivious. Everything that I have previously stated is true. Why else do you think I am here?"

"What do you—" I interrupt myself, unable to wrap my mind around the words dancing in the air between us. "What are you saying?"

"I am not here to help your friend."

My heart leaps up into my mouth. I stare at him in unbridled horror. Still, the logical part of my brain refuses to acknowledge the possibility that he might be right; instead, it begins to scream out that he's lying, that none of this is right and that the lunatic in front of me is most definitely not a Greek God. "Why are you here then?"

He holds me in a grave regard. "You know why I am here."

I breathe in so sharply that I almost faint, shaking my head repeatedly. "No. No. You can't. No. That isn't possible! You're not here to take him away. He doesn't deserve to die, not now. He can't. You're not here to take him away. You're not the god of the Underworld. Stop lying to me."

"Everyone dies at some point." Hades says. His words pierce through my defence like razor-sharp barbs. "His time just came earlier than others. It has nothing to do with what he deserves."

"Please!" A sob tears through my lips. When he doesn't respond, I glance down at my best friend's face. I break down when I catch his open eyes again, the complete lack of emotion in them setting the reality in stone. "You can't take him, not now! He's my best friend! Yes, he can be an ass, but he's the best thing in my life right now. I can't—" I shake my head, glaring up at him through my tears in defiance. "I won't let him die."

"I do not think you have a choice."

"Please!" I beg. He watches me, apathy shining out of his striking blue eyes. "You can't just let him die."

"I can't?" He smiles, just a little. I'm so gobsmacked by that small indication of humour that I'm surprised my eyes don't bug out like a typical cartoon character. "You just told me that I am neither the god of the Underworld nor that I possess the right to take him. Your argument does not make much sense."

"I know it doesn't! Nothing is making sense at the moment!" I clutch my head in my hands, looking around wildly. I can't accept the fact that my best friend is dead. I won't. My life had already been torn apart by the deaths of the people I knew and loved; I wasn't about to go and let my best friend fall victim to death too. "You can't be Hades. He's just a myth."

"That is flattering, but untrue. I am more than a myth." He holds up his hand. "But if you are still unsure of that fact, I will prove it to you."

He clicks his fingers and disappears from sight.

I just about fall over myself in my fright. I glance around wildly, momentarily forgetting all about my best friend as I try to find the dark stranger. Just as I'm working myself up into a frenzy, thick black clouds suddenly appear, roiling like molten lava and rumbling like thunder. The black clouds pulse around me until I'm completely surrounded, obscuring everything from my view so completely that it looks like all colour has been sucked from the world.

I catch a flicker of movement in the corner of my eye, and whirl around just in time to see Hades step out of the smoke. He watches me with a regard that sends icy shivers sliding down my spine.

"Do you believe me now?"

I stumble back, pointing a shaking finger at him. "Stop it. Stop messing with my head. Just stop. "

Hades walks forward until he's standing only a few feet in front of me. "I am not messing with your head. Everything that I am saying is the truth."

I swallow hard, his words ringing loud in my head.

"Then save him." I whisper. "If you are who you really say you are, then save him. Stop standing there and telling me he is dead. Bring him back, save him, do whatever the hell it is that you do. But don't you dare take him."

"It does not work like that." Hades replies sagely. Remorse flashes through his eyes so quickly that I almost miss it. "I cannot bring someone back from the dead that easily."

"But you can, right? You've done it in the past, I know you have." I demand, clenching my hands into fists at my sides. Everything that was happening was way too insane to be comprehensible, I knew that. But if there was a chance that I could save Spencer, no matter how insane or incomprehensible it was, I wasn't about to let it slip away from me. "Please, you have to tell me how. I'll do anything, anything to save him. He's my best friend."

"You'd do anything?" He echoes, surprise fleeting across his features. "Truly anything?"

I swallow, nodding without hesitation. "Of course I would. He doesn't deserve to die."

Hades watches me for several moments. When he finally speaks again, his voice is so quiet that it's almost unintelligible. "Have you heard of the story of Persephone?"

His question is so out of the blue that it momentarily stumps me. I blink in bewilderment.

"Of—Of course I have. Why?"

He continues to watch me impassively.

It sinks in.

"Oh. Oh." My eyes grow to the size of saucers. "You... you want me to come down to the Underworld? To sacrifice myself for his life?"

"Yes." Hades inclines his head. "If you descend to the Underworld with me for four months, I will prolong his death for a further four months."

"Only four months?" I stare at him in disbelief, shaking my head. "No. No way. Four months isn't fair."

"Even I cannot cheat death. I retain the ability to prolong the inevitable, but I cannot prevent death from happening altogether." Hades replies, his tone cool as ice. "Four months is what I am offering. Once you have stayed with me in the Underworld for four months, you will have four more months with Spencer before he dies. That is all I can do."

I bite my lip, indecision tearing through me. For the first time in my life, I was completely torn on what to do. Of course I knew the story of Persephone. It had been one of my favourite stories as a child; how she had been been kidnapped by Hades and dragged back down to the Underworld; how Demeter, distraught with grief at losing her daughter, had abandoned her duties as a goddess and searched the earth for her daughter, only to never find her; how it was too late when Demeter finally found her, because Persephone had eaten those four fated pomegranate seeds, and was forevermore forced to remain in the Underworld for four months every year — the months of winter. The Ancient Greeks had supposedly believed that myth to be the reason behind the colder seasons, but to believe that the myth of my childhood was actually a real story? And not only was it a real story, but I was expected to play the starring role in the modern rendition of it? My mind couldn't wrap itself around that concept at all, and the more I thought about it, the more I was filled with utter revulsion at the thought of being forced to leave with this stranger, to God knows where, for four months.

But then I look down at Spencer, and I'm hit with a barrage of memories. I remember all the fights and the pranks, all the cheeky smirks and drunken revelries, all the times that I couldn't forsake for the world. Suddenly, I couldn't imagine a future without that; and for the second time in a minute, I'm filled with revulsion again. Only this time, instead of at the stranger claiming to be a god, my revulsion is aimed at myself. If I didn't agree to his deal, and Spencer really did die, I would have to live with that for the rest of my life. I wouldn't have to agree to being willingly kidnapped, but I would have to live with the knowledge that that was only because I had been selfish enough to steal the rest of my best friend's life away from him, even if it was only for eight months. How would I ever be able to live with myself, knowing that I had been selfish enough to practically kill my best friend myself, all because I didn't want to take a chance?

The decision that I'd already unconsciously made becomes all the more clear. I clench my fingers into a fist, take a deep breath, and try my best not to think about the consequences of what I'm about to do.

"I'll do it."

Hades doesn't move a single muscle. He watches me carefully. "Are you sure that is your answer?"

"Yes. I'm sure."

"Very well." Hades nods minutely at me. Something that looks a lot like respect shines out of his eyes. "It is a very honourable decision, sacrificing yourself to save your friend. Not many would go that far for their friends."

I swallow and glance down at Spencer one last time, imprinting every crevice of his face into my mind. "No. It just makes me extremely stupid." Then I hesitate. "He'll be okay, right?"

"Of course. I may seem untrustworthy, but I never forsake a deal." Hades says seriously, holding out his arm. "Spencer will remain perfectly safe and healthy, both for the duration of our deal and for the four months you will have with him. That I can assure you."

He clicks his fingers, and, just like a movie being unpaused, the clouds surrounding us disappear and everything filters back into view. Hoards of people start pouring out of the mansion, Leia at the front of the crowd. Hair-raising screams quickly start to pierce the calm of the night as Spencer's motionless body is discovered, and I watch as more than one phone is whipped out. A small part of me wonders what on earth took them so long; it felt like Hades and I had been standing there talking for forever. But before I'm allowed to ponder on it anymore, a hand appears in my view. Swallowing hard, I tear my gaze away and step towards Hades, hesitantly touching his proffered hand.

And, just like that, everything around me changes in a blink, leaving behind the world I'd grown up in in a flash of darkness.

Chapter Four

C hapter Four

Less than a full second later, my feet stumble onto solid ground. My eyes fly open, and my mouth falls open with a quiet pop!. Gone was the raucous atmosphere, loud booming music and screaming patrons of the party, and in its place was the foyer of a giant, glittering palace, that looked like it had been stolen right out of Ancient Greece.

I twirl around in a big circle, taking in the spectacular beauty of the ancient building surrounding me. The white marble walls glisten under the warm light, like they're streaked with iridescent gold, and elegant white pillars frame the doorways, delicately etched with intricate designs. Winding around the edges of the room and up into the roof is a magnificent marble staircase, made from the same pearly marble as the walls. Monstrous diamond chandeliers dangle down from the roof like crystal waterfalls, scattering shadowy raindrops throughout the room. The clattering of my old boots echo against the white marble floors, and I suddenly feel extremely out of place.

My eyes widen as the realisation hits me. I cross my arms self-consciously over my body.

I've just agreed to be kidnapped by the god of the Underworld, and I'm wearing my pyjamas.

"Miss Autumn?"

I whirl around to see a young woman standing behind me, her hands folded behind her back. She looks to be around my age, with skin the colour of chocolate and long black curls twisted into an elaborate braid. Standing around her are three middle-aged men with varying appearances: one has cropped brunette hair and kind, twinkling eyes; the one in the middle, at least a head taller than his companions, has even shorter salt and pepper hair and a carefully manicured goatee; and the third one has wild, unmanned black curls, that appear even darker as he shrinks back into the shadows.

"Hi. Hello. You're all new." I blink in bewilderment and spin around again. "Where did he go?"

"Who?" The girl asks, confusion creasing her delicate features. "Hades?"

"Yes. Him. Where'd he go? I need to talk to him about..." I hesitate, twisting my lips to the side. Somehow I felt that I needed to talk to him about everything and nothing all at the same time. "Something?"

"He's gone. He doesn't tend to linger." The brunette man extends a hand and a warm smile. "Welcome to the Underworld, sweetheart."

"Cool it, Rhadamanthos. The girl has hardly been here for thirty seconds; she doesn't need to hear the reprehensible 'sweetheart' that's always dripping from your lips." The taller man in the middle rolls his eyes and steps forward. The young woman standing in front of him stumbles out of the way, her brow furrowing slightly. The man ignores her, nodding at me. "I am Minos. Welcome."

"Minos? As in King Minos of Crete? Of the Minotaur?" I gape. Minos shrugs nonchalantly, but his eyes glint smugly at my praise.

"You have heard of me, then?" He asks. He glances at Rhadamanthos out of the corner of his eye. "It is good to hear that at least my legacy lives on, isn't it brother?"

Rhadamanthos doesn't respond, but his jaw tightens almost imperceptibly. He keeps his gaze fixed on me and smiles a bright, beaming smile.

"As my brother has already betrayed, my name is Rhadamanthos, and his Minos. Over there is Aeacus, the silent partner in our trio."

My gaze follows his finger and I squeak out a star-struck, "Hello."

Aeacus doesn't respond, keeping his dark eyes firmly locked on the door. I falter.

"Is he..."

"Don't mind him. He prefers four legs over two." Minos waves his hand, recapturing my attention. Simultaneously, both he and Rhadamanthos bow and step back. "We will get out of your hair and allow your maid to show you your room."

"My room?" I frown. "Why do I have my own - oh."

The young woman waits in front of me patiently, ignoring the way my expression drops. "If you would come with me, Miss Autumn?"

My heart sinks. This is happening. This is actually happening. Spencer actually died, the god of the Underworld actually offered to make a deal with me to save his life, and I actually... agreed? And now I'm standing in a palace. In the Underworld. If I knew any better, I'd probably laugh at the absurdity of it all. Me, Evie Autumn, in the Underworld, after being spirited away by Hades? That's the stuff of daydreams.

Or, more realistically, nightmares.

The young woman clears her throat. "Miss Autumn? Are you ready for me to take you to your room? Hades will find you when he's ready, you have my assurance."

"Yes, I suppose he will." I reply with a sigh, my shoulders slumping. I glance up and shoot her a small smile. "I guess I'm ready, then."

She nods and, without another word, briskly walks out of the foyer. I hasten to catch up with her. The halls clatter with the sound of our hurried footsteps, further emphasising the immensity and emptiness of the palace I'd just been spirited off to.

I clear my throat. "So. The Underworld. We're in the Underworld."

The woman keeps her gaze fixed ahead. "If that is what you prefer to call it, yes."

"And that man I arrived with, he's... he's Hades. A god." I hesitate, my mind struggling to accept the word. It feels incredibly peculiar, rolling off my tongue like a big gobstopper. "A god."

She briefly looks back at me, smiling minutely. "It takes a little getting used to, I know."

"'A little getting used to'? You're kidding right?" I laugh a little, rubbing my head with my hand. "This is all ridiculous. It's more than ridiculous, it's crazy. Far too much crazy to take in before ten in the morning."

"Don't worry. You'll have four months to get used to it." She tells me, turning down a small corridor.

The words echo through my mind the same way our footsteps echo through the palace, and my step falters as reality hits me hard. Four months. Four months. I'm really here for four whole months. I didn't get a chance to say goodbye to Minnie. Or the twins. Or Spencer. And now I won't see them again for four months.

Tears prick the corners of my eyes. I didn't even get to say goodbye.

"Miss Autumn?" The girl touches my shoulder, her expression concerned. "Are you okay?"

"Not at all." I wipe my eyes with the back of my hand and flash her a faltering smile. "And it's Evie. If you keep calling me Miss Autumn I think I'll kill someone. It's far too formal for my liking."

"Miss Autumn-" She checks herself, blushing, and giggles sheepishly. "Evie. That's an empty threat around here."

"Right. The Underworld. Place of the Dead." I laugh, running a hand through my messy strawberry-blonde curls. "What's your name? You have a name, right?"

"Of course I have a name. It's Calla." She pushes open a door and holds it for me, gesturing me through. "Your room, Evie."

Wrapping my arms around myself protectively, I hesitantly walk past her and enter my room for the next four months. For the second time in five minutes, my mouth drops open. The exquisitely decorated master bedroom that greets me takes me completely by surprise - I was half expecting to walk into a stone cold jail cell, not a bedroom fit for a queen. To my left, a huge four-poster bed sits proudly, the posts carved into twisting tree branches that spiral up into an intertwined canopy of branches and leaves. A plush turquoise sofa rests against the opposite wall on an angle, facing the biggest television screen I've ever seen in my life. And tucked behind the sofa is a door, adjar just enough to reveal a sparkling white marble bathroom, equipped with a glittering open shower and a jacuzzi the size of a small pool.

"I'm supposed to return in precisely an hour and a half." Calla's soft voice interrupts my astounded gawking. I jolt, turning to see her standing demurely behind me. "Hades informed me you will want some time alone, but he has requested that you attend a meal with him tonight."

"A meal?" I frown. "I didn't realise that my imprisonment included me attending meals with him."

"Evie." Her expression softens with sympathy. "Do not think of this as an imprisonment. He does not want you to think of it that way. You did agree to come willingly."

"Because he forced me to make a deal with him." I point out. "It may have been my decision to agree to his deal, but I didn't really have a choice."

"You always have a choice." The words burst out of her mouth before she can stop them. I blink, taken aback by the sudden outburst, and Calla's face blanches. She clears her throat and looks down at her feet, mumbling, "He's not a bad person, you know. You just have to get to know him to see that."

"He's the god of the dead." I reply tightly. "So forgive me if I don't believe you at this point in time, but I do have a rather tinted view of him at the moment. I don't want to get to know him."

"Don't believe all the stories you hear. And don't blame him for a decision you made." Calla walks over to the door, and pauses, glancing back at me over her shoulder. "I'll be back in an hour and a half to get you ready."

I don't respond, watching in silence as she walks out and pulls the door shut behind her. The second the door clicks shut, my shoulders slump, and I fall onto the bed. All the euphoria that I felt at the sight of my room dissipates into thin air. Suddenly, all I want to do is curl up into a ball, squeeze my eyes shut and forget everything that's happening, like I used to do when I was a child and reality had gotten too much.

I let out a shaky breath and slowly lay back on the plush maroon comforter, staring up at the ceiling. The diamond chandelier sways gently above me, the light skittering across the roof like millions of tiny stars. The tips of the diamond are stained in an ombre from light to midnight blue, creating the illusion of small raindrops falling from the ceiling. I smile slightly. I'd always loved the rain. I could remember the countless times I'd lain in bed, or curled up on the window-seat of my parents' lounge, with a book notched in my lap as I listened to the rain pattering across the roof. No other sound was quite as calming or relaxing to me, and calming and relaxing was definitely in short supply right now.

My gaze skims around the room, following the path of the stars. My frown deepens. If I didn't know better, I'd almost say that this room was designed for me, and me exclusively. From the assortment of cushions peppering the king-sized bed right down to the thick red shag rug blanketing a large part of the room's floor, it was the bedroom I'd always dreamed about - when I'd allowed myself to indulge in such expensive dreams.

Only, I'd never really dreamed about it being in the Underworld.

Talk about irony.

I swallow several times. Tears well up in my eyes as my mind ricochets back to the people I'd left behind. I'd barely been away from them for an hour, and I was already missing them: how pathetic was that? If I couldn't survive an hour away from them, how in the world was I supposed to survive four whole months?

A knock sounds at my door, tearing me out of my dark thoughts. I sit up, hastily wiping my cheeks. "Come in."

The door swings open to reveal Hades.

He steps into my room, his expression impassive. I sit up even straighter and clear my throat, tucking my hair behind my ears.

"Hi."

"You're sad." He states it as factually as one does when they're talking about the weather.

"Yes." I blink, momentarily taken aback, before reassembling my defences in the form of biting sarcasm. "Thank you for that insightful observation, Captain Obvious."

"Why are you sad?" He asks, walking forward to stand in front of me.

"I would think the answer to that question was just as obvious."

Hades sighs, his blank expression wavering for a moment. "I am sorry you are sad. That was not my intention."

"What was your intention then?" I ask, protectively crossing my arms as I stand up. "To make me happy by giving me an impossible choice? Either way, I was going to end up heartbroken, no matter what I decided. You had to know that."

"That was not my intention either." He tells me. My face crumples up in confusion.

"Well then what was your intention, Hades?" I demand, pushing myself up onto my toes so I can look him dead in the eye. "What do you want from me?"

"I only want your happiness for the duration of your stay here." Hades steps back, putting space between us again. If I didn't know better, I'd say something that looks uncannily like pain flashes through his eyes. "Nothing more."

"Yes. Well," I clear my throat and look away. "We both know that isn't going to happen."

He stays silent. My heart sinks. Up until that very moment, a part of me had still held out the small ridiculous hope that he wouldn't actually hold me to this deal, that he'd take me home and be kind-hearted enough to keep up his end of the deal and keep Spencer alive. But Hades' deafening silence shreds that hope into obliteration.

Another, more idiotic part of me held out the even smaller, even more ridiculous hope that this was all a dream, that if I just closed my eyes I'd wake up in the safety of my bed. I gaze down at my hands and curl my fingers into my palms, biting my lip to cut off the squeak of pain that rises up when my nails pierce the skin.

Well that settles it then. Definitely not a dream either. So that leaves...

Reality.

This is my new reality.

Silently, I steel myself. I needed to stop acting like the damsel-in-distress. I wouldn't achieve anything if I continued to pity myself. If I was going to be stuck here for the next four months, I might as well familiarise myself with my new reality; with the god I made the deal with in the first place, and with the world that I had thought was preserved safely in the stories of mythology. I didn't have to like Hades - given the circumstances, I had high doubts that I ever would like him - but I would be stupid if I didn't try to get a feel for the kind of person he was. He was a god, after all. I wasn't about to let him smite me because I accidentally ended up pissing him off.

I look back up at Hades. Only this time, I really look at him. I'd like to say I've always been a good judge of character, been able to figure out what type of person someone was just by looking at them. But, as hard as I study Hades, I can't see past the surface - I can't break past his mask of frigid indifference. He's a complete closed book. My curiosity piques. I broach the silence.

"I didn't expect any of this."

Surprise fleets across his features, momentarily shattering his poker face. "Any of what?"

I motion to my room. "This. My room. The palace. I didn't expect the Underworld to be so... light."

"The Underworld has many names, and, with those names, many associated connotations that are entirely inaccurate. It is not the 'hell' that many of those names lead people to believe. Its proper name is Elysium."

"Elysium? Like the Elysian Fields?"

Hades raises his eyebrows. "You know quite a lot about mythology."

I shrug, keeping my voice light. "A little."

The corners of his mouth turn up slightly. "The ancient Greeks were the most correct, out of all the civilisations, in their beliefs of what Elysium represented. What they did not get right, however, was the very structure of Elysium."

"The structure?"

"Elysium becomes whatever a person thinks they deserve when they die. If they think they deserve to end up in a golden world, populated by angels with wings, then that is where they end up. If they think they deserve to be eternally punished for their sins, then that is what happens." Hades explains. My eyes widen in understanding. "If a person is unsure of what they deserve, or they think they deserve an afterlife that I believe to be unjust, then it is up to my judges or myself to step in. It is all a judgement system based on the individual's morality and their own perception of themselves. Does that make sense?"

"I think so." I reply slowly. "But why the palace? How does that fit in?"

"I am the King of the Underworld." Hades says simply. "All kings deserve a palace. I just created it to look the way I wanted it to. Unfortunately, once you pass the boundaries of the palace, the landscape is a little more revealing of the nature of Elysium. I do suggest you refrain from crossing those boundaries at all costs, should you wish to avoid an encounter with an ungrateful wraith."

"Okay. That's understandable." I tilt my head from side to side in acknowledgement. "Why are you telling me this?"

"Why are you asking?"

I smile at him, bitterness leaking into my expression. "I'm going to be stuck here for four months. Might as well know what my home for the next four months is like, right?"

Hades doesn't reply, but his expression turns glacial at the flip of a switch. The temperature in the room drops several degrees. He turns on his heel, reaching for the door. "The meal is in 3 hours. I expect to see you there. You will be, as you say, stuck there too, until I deem otherwise." He hovers at the door fleetingly, looking at me over his shoulder. "I like the penguins, but I suspect my dinner guests may not. I suggest you change before my return."

I look down at my pyjama bottoms and flush scarlet. By the time I look back up again, he's gone.

- - -

It doesn't take long for me to grow bored of sitting on my bed, with only my thoughts to keep me company, so I make the executive decision to explore my room. I open all the cupboard doors, barely suppressing a squeal of excitement when I unearth the biggest walk-in closet in the world. I pointlessly run water into the jacuzzi, watching the mountain of bubbles the powerful jets create grow with unadulterated fascination. I even indulge in my childish fantasies and jump on the bed, melting into the cloud-like maroon comforter when my legs turn into jelly. At one point, I even try to explore outside my room - but the second I take two steps towards the door, the door handle disappears into the dark mahogany wood. That little discovery cut straight through the elegantly woven illusion, and removed all sense of adventure from me as effectively as a slap to the face.

When Calla knocks on my door exactly an hour and a half after she left, I'm lying on the couch with my feet hanging over the edge, mindlessly flipping through the television channels as I silently stew in my frustration.

"Miss Evie?"

"Here." I reply monotonously, holding my hand up so she can see me. I push myself up to a sitting position and narrow my eyes at her. "I have a question."

"Yes?" She stands in front of the television, hands folded in front of her.

"How is it," I wave the television remote at her. "That the Underworld has thousands of television channels? It's the Underworld. It doesn't make any logical sense."

"This is your part of Elysium." Calla tells me. "It functions however you want it to - including access to television channels, should you wish it."

"However I want it ?" I stand up and fold my arms, my lips twisted up sourly. "If it works however I want it to, then why did the door handle disappear when I tried to leave?"

Calla falters, her brown eyes widening. "I don't know, Miss Evie."

"He will." I say bluntly. Calla's skin pales. "Hades. He'll know, won't he?"

"I don't know, Miss Evie." She blanches even more under my heavy gaze and starts stuttering. "I-I need to get you ready. For the dinner. Hades has insisted upon it."

"The dinner?" For a moment, I have no idea what she's talking about. But then I remember. "Oh. The dinner." I glance down at my feet, kicking my left heel against my toes. "What if I don't want to go?"

"Then he will be quite angry. So very angry." Calla whispers, looking so frightened that my frustration melts away. "Please do not make me the cause of that anger."

"Alright." I hold my hands up, a little alarmed by the thinly-veiled terror behind her eyes. "Alright, I'm sorry. I'll go. It'll give me the chance to ask him why my room is keeping me imprisoned, anyway."

The relief that had started to spread across Calla's expression shrivels up and blackens at my statement.

"Please don't." She begs softly. "He'll be so-"

"Angry. You've said. I'm not afraid of him, Calla." I say, perching on the arm of the sofa and watching as she walks over to the walk-in wardrobe.

"That's because you haven't seen him while he's angry." Calla responds quietly, flinching and glancing over her shoulder fearfully the moment the words leave her lips. She eyes the door for a moment, almost as if she's expecting Hades to burst through it and chew her out for her honesty. After a few more Hades-less seconds, her shoulders slump in relief, and she shakes herself as a new energy revitalises her. Breezing past me, she opens up the wardrobe and rifles through it. After several seconds, she lets out a small exclamation and pulls out a cream dress that has far too many ruffles and a very suspicious looking corset. I immediately hold my hands up.

"No. No. Absolutely not." I protest. She gives me a look. "I don't care how formal this dinner is, I'd rather go in my pyjamas than in that Victorian death trap."

"This is not a death trap!" Calla insists. "All the girls I knew wore these all the time!"

I stare at her. "How old are you?"

"Twenty-three." She tells me matter-of-factly, reluctantly hanging the dress back in the wardrobe. I blink several times, completely bewildered, but she doesn't elaborate. Calla sighs, puffing out her cheeks and looking back at me with a torn expression. "If you don't wear something he approves of, it will be on my head."

I groan. "Don't give me that look. Then I'll feel bad, and I'll end up in one of those dresses."

She doesn't reply. If anything, her pout grows even bigger. I let out a long sigh and throw my hands up in defeat.

"Fine. I'll wear a dress, but only," I hold up a finger and give her a look. "If you find one that's a little closer to the century I was born in."

Calla beams at me and nods, turning back to the wardrobe again. After muttering to herself for a few more seconds, her nimble fingers flitting past a rainbow of dresses, Calla finally lets out a triumphant exclamation and pulls a dress out of the rainbow. A grin ricochets over my lips.

"That's more like it."

"Good." Calla carefully lays the strapless seafoam ball-dress on my bed, before spinning around and clicking her fingers at me. "Take off your clothes."

"Excuse me?" A surprised laugh tumbles out of my lips. "I'm sorry, you're pretty and all, but I just don't swing that way."

"That is not what I meant, Miss Evie." Calla rolls her eyes at my joke, her brown eyes twinkling. "Are you going to wear your evening garments underneath the dress?"

"Well... No."

"Precisely. So go to the bathroom. There are undergarments waiting for you there." She tells me, waving her hands. "Then I can put you in your dress and send you on your way."

"You know, you're not exactly acting like a twenty-three year old. I don't like it." I grumble, grudgingly standing up and walking to the bathroom. Calla just laughs.

One hour, thirty-seven minutes and fifteen seconds later, Calla finally reaches the point where she deems me 'ready'. I, on the other hand, reach the point of having my hair pulled and teased that minute too long, and was struggling more and more to resist falling into the mountain of blankets and cushions behind me.

"Calla, what's the probability that I will be the target of a particular god's anger if I don't turn up to this dinner?" I ask, making a face as I appraise my appearance in the bathroom mirror. As much as I hated the whole experience of being dressed up to the nines, I don't exactly hate the result. The seafoam dress is simple and elegant, with a swooping sweetheart neckline, elegant drop-shoulder sleeves, and flowing skirts that fall down in a silky waterfall. It flatters me in all the right places, and makes me seem a lot taller than my 5"7 frame really is.

The dark-haired girl appears at my shoulder. Her reflection smiles sweetly at me, a cat-like glint flickering through her eyes. "It will not be the anger of just one god. It will be the anger of several gods and one handmaiden."

"Handmaiden?" I whirl around to frown at her. "You're my handmaiden?"

"Of course." She replies sagely, rearranging my curls back. "Who did you think I was?"

"Well, I don't know..." I shrug slightly, a small smile curling up my lips. "My friend?"

Calla falters. A soft knock sounds on my bedroom door. She jumps, her eyes widening.

"That will be Hades, Miss Autumn. I will go get him."

"Wait, Calla-"

She disappears before I can get another word in edgewise. Hades materialises in her place. I gasp, and instinctively throw the closest thing to me. He barely manages to catch the soap dispenser I send flying through the air before it shatters against the wall. My cheeks catch fire.

"Um. Hi." I lean against the bathroom wall, slip, and resort to folding my arms over my chest. I clear my throat. "Hi. Hello."

He inclines his head once in response. "Are you ready to go?"

"Go where?" I raise an eyebrow at him. "It's a little hard to go anywhere when the door handle disappears every time you try to leave the room."

Hades doesn't say anything. I plough on, unable to stop myself.

"Why does it do that, by the way? I thought you said I wasn't a prisoner here."

"You are not." Hades tells me softly. Always softly, always quietly, always without emotion.

"Why did the door handle disappear then?" I ask, tucking my hands under my armpits so he doesn't see them shaking with frustration. "I know I agreed to your deal Hades, but if I'm going to survive down here then you need to give me some freedom. You can't expect me to be okay with you keeping me locked in my room for four whole months, and I'll tell you right now, if you do, I'm probably going to go mad, and you don't want to see me when I've gone mad. Spencer has told me on multiple occasions that I look like an angry chipmunk when I have and - oh my god, I'm babbling, aren't I?" I cut myself off and cover my mouth with my hand, staring at Hades in horror.

Hades smiles, looking like he's holding back a laugh, and nods once. I narrow my eyes at him.

"Don't laugh at me, I'm trying to make a point here." I retort. Hades clears his throat, blinking once to prove his reproachfulness.

"I apologise. What were you saying?"

I bite my lip to stop a smile from breaking out onto my face. "Look, I made a deal with you, and I'm not about to break it. So can you please just trust me, and not lock me in my room? Please?"

Hades hesitates for a moment, before inclining his head. My shoulders relax.

"Very well. I will make sure all the doors within the palace are unlocked, so long as you promise me you will not leave the palace. I may trust you, but I do not trust those that exist outside the walls."

"That sounds fair." I nod, allowing a small smile. "Thank you."

"You are welcome." Hades replies, holding out his arm. "Now if you are ready, we must get going. My guests will not wait forever."

"Okay." I swallow and hesitantly place my palm on his forearm. Hades nods at me again and leads me out of my room. I wince as my stilettos clatter against the polished floors, creating an unnecessarily aggressive echo as we head down the hallway. Hades, on the other hand, glides alongside me silently, his shoes making no sound on the marble floors. I try not to scowl too sullenly.

Thanks for that, Calla. You couldn't have just put me in converse like I told you to.

"So um," I clear my throat, looking up at him. "Why am I going to this dinner exactly? And who are your guests?"

"My family." Hades tells me impassively, keeping his gaze fixed ahead.

"Your family?"

He nods. "While we are not technically biologically related, they are the closest thing I have to a family, dysfunctional as it may be."

"What do you mean, you're not biologically related?"

He looks down at me, an eyebrow raised. "I thought you said you knew Greek mythology?"

"I do, but if they're your family, then that would mean..." I stop, my eyes widening in realisation. Oh. Duh, Evie. "We're meeting the other gods?"

"Yes." Hades replies, leading me up to two big golden doors. Behind the doors, I can hear the faint murmur of voices. Many voices, in fact. I falter, paling a little. "Are you ready?"

"Ready?" I gulp, my grip on his wrist tightening. "I'm about to walk into a room full of real life, breathing-the-same-air-as-me gods and goddesses, and you're asking me if I'm ready?"

"You have already met one. I think you are doing fine." He tells me, surprising a laugh out of me.

"Dear god, what has my life become?"

"Who exactly are you talking to?"

I quirk my eyebrows at him. "Oh, so now the King of the Dead is sassing me?"

He chuckles, the sound low and melodic. "You will be fine, Evie."

I blink. That's the first time he's said my name since I made the deal with him. For some strange reason, that small acknowledgement is incredibly comforting. "Okay."

"Very well."

Without another word, he pushes the golden doors open and leads me into the brightly lit room. The murmur of voices abruptly stop, and several heads swivel simultaneously to look at us. I swallow hard, gripping Hades' arm in a vice-like grip. I may have only met the man a few hours ago, but he's the only deity I know in this entire room, and that's enough to have me clinging to him like a scared child.

I keep my eyes fixed on my shoes as we walk past all the gods and goddesses, feeling the sharp pinpricks of their gazes on my back as we glide by. I start chewing on the inside of my cheek.

I don't like this. I don't like this at all. Please tell me it's over.

"Look up." Hades murmurs in my ear. "Or they will think you do not want to look at them."

"I don't." I mumble. He chuckles, nudging me with his elbow. I swallow back the golf ball lodged in my throat and grudgingly obey him, timidly glancing up at the crowd of people watching us.

And the faces that I see before me are so painfully familiar that they just about floor me. My heart stops.

No.

Chapter Five

C hapter Five

"Evie?" Hades touches my elbow, attempting to pull me forward. I don't budge.

"No." I stare straight ahead, wide-eyed in horror. Pure ice pulses through my veins, freezing me to the spot and eradicating all semblance of movement from my muscles.

"Evie." My name is said a second time, this time by a different person. The sound of my name tumbling off their lips is like a stab in the back. I stagger, my knees struggling to keep me standing.

I lick my lips several times and point a quivering hand at them. "No. No. This isn't happening. Please tell me this isn't happening."

Not a single one of them says a word, guilt clear on their faces. Selene. Axel. Minnie. Olly. Spencer. Even Leia stands behind Spencer. Every single person I've ever known, or come to love, since the death of my family stands right before me, in a situation that I'm not sure I want to believe. All of a sudden the floor feels like it's being pulled out from underneath me, slowly dissipating into thin air and dropping me screaming into an abyss of oblivion. Stumbling back, I grab onto the nearest thing to me — which just so happens to be Hades — and stare at them, my heart thudding against my ribcage.

No.

"You." I point at Spencer. "You—you're dead. How are you here? You can't be here. You're dead."

"Evie..." He steps forward, his face twisted with remorse. I step back, and pain flashes through his eyes. "E, please, I can explain."

"No. Stop it. Just stop it." I shake my head, my mind refusing to let itself accept the facts being presented to it. "Why are you here?"

"Evie." Hades finally speaks up, forcing me to look at him. He gives me a pointed look. "Who did I say we were meeting?"

"You—your family. The other gods." I shake my head again, feeling like it's full of cotton wool. "But that would mean... no. No. That's not right. It can't be right. That means that—" I look back at Spencer, my family, and my heart sinks. "No."

"Evie—" Spencer tries again.

"No. Stop it." Shaking my head repetitively now, I cross my arms over my chest. My breathing intensifies. My whole body starts shaking uncontrollably, my head spinning as the world tilts on its axis. "This doesn't make any sense. You were dead, Spencer. You died. How are you standing in front of me?"

"You know why Evie." He says quietly. "I'm sorry you had to find out this way, I really am. I told him you weren't ready, but unfortunately he," He glares hotly at Hades. "Didn't listen to me."

Hades narrows his eyes slightly at Spencer. The temperature in the room drops.

"But you died." I say weakly, tears pricking at the corners of my eyes. "I watched you die."

"You watched my mortal body die." Spencer explains, his words twisted with bitterness. "But not my true form. I can't die that easily in my true form. You know that."

I swallow and shakily glance over at my foster family. They all meet my gaze with expressions that vary in degrees of solemnity. Selene even has the audacity to look apologetic. But they still remain silent.

"So you're all gods." I state. Silence. I nod several times, my arms tightening across my chest. It feels like that's my only protection against the swarm of lies surrounding me. "Who are you really, then? Hades prefers his Greek name, and I bet you all do too. So stop standing there saying nothing and tell me."

"Artemis." Selene says, shooting me a remorseful smile.

"Apollo." Axel adds on. I laugh sardonically. Of course. How did I not realise?

"Athena." Minnie sighs, suddenly looking much older. "I'm sorry, Evie. We weren't trying to deceive you. It was all for your well-being, I promise."

"Sure it was. Forgive me if I don't believe you." I retort. I look at Spencer, speaking sharply. "And who are you? Dionysus?"

He somehow manages to grin in the situation. "How did you guess?"

"Unbelievable." I snort, gripping my arms so tightly that I can practically feel my skin bruising. "I'm sorry. This is just—"

My sentence dies in my throat when I look over at Hades. He meets my gaze, his expression as emotionless as ever. I shake my head again, slowly backing up.

"I'm sorry. I can't do this. I have to... I have to go."

Before anyone has a chance to stop me, I walk out of the room as fast as I can, my breathing erratic. Even without looking at them, I know that every single person in that room is watching me as I run out with my tail between my legs. But I couldn't care less. All that flashes through my mind is the faces that I thought I knew; all that I could hear was the lies they'd been telling me half of my life. They all probably thought it was hilarious, pushing me to pursue my obsession with Greek mythology, all the while knowing that I was just learning all about them. It was the worst kind of narcissistic complex, and they had all encouraged it.

Squeezing my eyes shut, I fall back against the wall and slowly slide down to the ground, pinching the bridge of my nose. Just like that, I had lost all sense of what's real. From the moment my family died, I had spent my whole life living a perfectly formed lie, and I was struggling to find the fixed points of reality in it. How could I, when I'd been brought up by characters from mythology?

"Evie."

I startle and glance up, wiping the tears off my cheeks. Hades stands before me, his hands shoved into the pockets of his black trench-coat. When he notices the state I'm in, chagrin flashes across his features. Realisation slaps me in the face. Suddenly, everything makes sense.

"It was all you." I whisper. "I ran into you at the airport. And then when Spencer was on the phone... it was you he was talking to, wasn't it? It was you he told I wasn't ready."

Hades nods. I swallow hard and push myself up to my feet.

"Did you plan all of this?" A horrific thought hits me. My heart clenches painfully. "Did you... did you kill my family too?"

"No." Hades tells me. "Of course not. I first noticed you when I helped your parents transition."

"My parents? You saw my parents?" I look at him in horror. "How?"

He sighs, running a hand through his ashen hair. "That is what I do, Evie. I am the Lord of the Dead. I help people transition into their afterlives."

"Then why were you so interested in me? I'm not dead, I'm completely and utterly alive; so why did you fixate on me? Why did you think you had the right to raise me on lies?"

"I cannot tell you."

"Seriously? Seriously?" I laugh humorlessly, throwing my hands up in the air. "Your explanation for all the lies is that you can't tell me? What, are you also going to tell me now that I'm dreaming, or—or—or that I'm overreacting, that I should be taking this all in stride? How does Persephone deal with this, with all the lying and the secrets?"

"She does not." Hades says shortly, his tone so cold that it makes me blink and stop short. "You are not dreaming, nor are you overreacting."

"Well, then why won't you tell me why you decided to control my life, Hades?" I exclaim, gesturing wildly. "I deserve to know why you thought it would be a good idea to have a group of primordial beings raise me like their pet human!"

"I do not act without a good reason, Evie." Hades says seriously. "You may not have the highest opinion of me right now, but I meant it when I say that I am not fond of lying or keeping secrets. I did not lie when we made the deal, did I? Spencer is still alive."

"Because he's a god!" I yell, my tone bordering on hysterical. Hades responds with yet more silence. My words echo through my mind. I pause as a realisation occurs to me. "He's a god. Which means he... he can't die if I break off the deal, can he?"

Hades stills. "No."

"So I could break off the deal."

"Yes." He says impassively. "I was under the impression, however, that you did not break your promises."

"I... I don't." I stammer, leaning my head back against the wall. "But you tricked me into agreeing to your terms. You orchestrated for him to die, right in front of me, so I agreed to your deal. I was tricked into this all along."

"I may have organised the premise of the situation, but I did not orchestrate your reaction. You had every right to say no to me, to let your friend die, but you did not. You sacrificed yourself for him, and that is the reason I offered you the deal in the first place. You are extremely unique, Evie. Not many mortals would actually agree to that deal in the first place."

"That still doesn't change the fact that I was tricked into this, Hades. I may have agreed to your deal, but you can't possibly think that it was a fair one."

Hades lets out a long breath and inclines his head in agreement. "I will admit that the circumstances under which the deal was presented were unfair, and I apologise for that. If you really feel that you cannot stay here for the duration of the deal, then you may leave. I will not stop you."

With that, he turns and starts to walk away. I watch him go in silence. Confusion clouds my mind. I can't ignore the fact that what he did was wrong and unfair, and a small part of me can't help thinking that I should take up his offer without a second thought. It was what I'd been wishing for all along, after all. Besides which, I should be cursing him for being the reason that the only people left alive that I love are gods: gods who are immortal, gods who will outgrow me and gods who will, one day, watch me die.

But somehow, despite that, when I look at him, all my anger disappears. Left in its place is sympathy: sympathy for the quiet, dark god in front of me. He may have just turned my life upside-down for some secret reason, but I couldn't help feeling sorry for him, and my curiosity wasn't letting me leave that feeling alone. Besides which, Hades was right about one thing: I had made a deal with him, and I never broke my deals unless I had a really good reason to. And even if I did break it, and returned to my old life, there would be nothing waiting for me. My family, all my friends, would be gone. I'd be all alone, all over again. And the thought of that, the thought of having to start all over again, was just that bit more painful than staying.

I sigh, biting my lip. "Wait."

Hades pauses, but doesn't turn around.

"I'm sorry." I blow out my cheeks and take a couple of steps forward. "You're right. I said I never break my deals, and I don't. Me breaking my deals when I say I don't break deals is technically me breaking a deal, and I told you I wouldn't do that. But that's not important."

I take a deep breath, cutting myself off before I ramble on too much.

"What I'm trying to say is, I'll give it a go. Staying down here, I mean. I did make a deal with you, after all."

He turns his head to the side ever so slightly. "If you desire to leave, then you are more than welcome to."

"I don't." I reply, shrugging my shoulders. "Well, I don't think I want to. Not at the moment, anyway. I just said it before because I was... confused, I guess. I tend to think aloud when I'm confused."

I hear him sigh quietly. His shoulder slumps. "I do not want to force you to be here, Evie. I do not want you to be unhappy. I will not make that mistake again."

Mistake? Again? What does he mean by that?

I open my mouth to ask him, but stop. Focus, Evie. "If you don't lie to me, don't keep secrets from me, and treat me like an equal, not a prisoner, then I won't be unhappy. It's only for four months, isn't it?"

"Yes. Four months."

"Then that's how long I'm here for. Four months." I swallow, nodding with what I hope is convincing finality. If I can convince everyone else, then maybe I can convince myself too.

Hades doesn't respond, but I can tell from the small shift in his stance that he heard me. After a few more beats of silence, I walk up to him and hesitantly touch his shoulder.

"I have just one more question. Well, two actually."

He turns, eyebrows raised. "Yes?"

"Can I not go back there? Like, ever again?" I ask timidly, my fingers twisting around themselves. "I don't think I can face going back in there and pretending everything is okay over chicken and peas."

"I can assure you that it would not be over chicken and peas," Hades replies, a hint of bemusement in his tones. "But I am sure they will understand your absence, given the circumstances. What was your other question?"

I clear my throat, trying not to let my voice shake. "Can I... can I see my parents?"

The moment Hades hears my request, surprise flashes across his face; but the emotion is gone just as fleetingly as it came. He shakes his head.

"I am sorry Evie, but I cannot grant that request. While I may be able to excuse you from the dinner, I will not have as much luck for myself. My family will not take well to the host of the dinner leaving."

"Oh." I try not to let the disappointment show on my face. Instead, I hold onto the fact that he didn't outright say no; that there was the possibility that I might be able to see them sometime soon, if not now. "Okay."

"Is that all?" Hades asks. I nod mutely. He inclines his head. "Very well. Calla will come and show you to your room."

Hades disappears as soon as he's finished his sentence, leaving his words to ring all around me as I stand alone in the hallway of the Underworld's palace.

— — —

Much to my chagrin, I didn't see Hades — or any of the other gods — for an entire month following what I dubbed the 'disaster-dinner'. I don't know why that came as such a surprise to me, though. The Underworld wasn't exactly famous for its parties and cheeriness, nor was it exactly a popular holiday destination, so it shouldn't have come as a shock that Spencer, or the twins, or even Minnie hadn't visited.

That still didn't stop their sudden disappearance from hurting, though.

Despite my resentment towards them for lying, I didn't want them permanently severed from my life. All I needed was time to process it all, to try and figure out what the hell my life had become, not complete and utter abandonment; but it seems that Hades had really taken my request to heart. The handful of times I'd seen Spencer and Olly walking through the immense palace in the Underworld, they'd both blanched and quickly ducked round a corner, gone before I managed to catch up with them. And that hurt a lot more than I wanted it to.

Hades, on the other hand, I didn't see at all. Not a fleeting glimpse, or a shadow, or even a whisper. He had, for all appearances, completely disappeared into thin air, and become nothing more than the myth fashioned from the mouths of the ancient Greeks. More than once, I almost gave into believing that he was that literary creation, rather than the actual person I had met. Had it not been for the look of terror on Calla's face whenever I so much as suggested doing anything that he might not approve of, I probably would have. For the first time in my life, I was completely and utterly alone, and the more time that passed without a single interaction with the man who had literally turned my life upside-down, the more I started to feel like maybe I had descended into literal hell.

To distract myself, I spent most of my time exploring the palace, with the goal to discover as many rooms as I possibly could. Calla, who had quickly become my one and only friend, found my plight incredibly amusing, particularly the expression of complete bewilderment I made when the room I'd just been exploring disappeared the moment I stepped out of the door.

Then, exactly one month and six days after I made the deal with Hades, I'm sprawled over my couch, lazily watching a movie, when a quiet knock sounds on my door. Frowning, I pause the movie and slowly sit up, staring at the innocent wooden partition. I'd previously told Calla she could just let herself in whenever she arrived, considering she was here almost all the time; it had even taken me almost half an hour to convince her that it was actually fine. But apart from Calla, nobody ever came to see me. My frown deepens.

So who on earth was on the other side of the door?

"Hello?" I cross my room and pull open the door. I stop short when I see the person on the other side. "Oh. Hi."

"Hello." Hades nods, watching me with his usual impassive gaze.

"Um…" I clear my throat, tucking my hair behind my ear and folding my arms over my chest. At least this time, I'm wearing something more decent than my scrappy old penguin pyjamas. As well as being my maidservant, I'd quickly discovered that Calla was also in charge of my wardrobe — something we had quarrelled over several times. At the beginning, she had been near-on determined to stuff me in dresses that had me in a perpetual state of breathlessness and just general pain, but after I finally put my foot down and threatened to strike by walking around butt-naked, she grudgingly gave in and started offering up more modern wardrobe options. As much as I loved Victorian dresses, they were hell to walk around in comfortably — particularly if you'd been exploring a palace as obsessively as I'd been. "Not to be blunt, but I haven't seen you for an entire month. Why are you suddenly talking to me now?"

"I apologise for that." Hades replies sagely. "I have been much busier than anticipated. I did not mean to leave you alone in such an abrupt manner."

"You didn't." I shrug. "Calla's been keeping me company. She's been watching me make a fool out of myself exploring the different corners of the palace. Did you know that there is a room that has one hundred cellos in it? One hundred cellos. I was so bored that I counted them all. But then the room disappeared, and now I've kind of become obsessed with finding the room of one hundred cellos. Did I mention there were one hundred cellos?"

His eyebrows raise. "Calla has been accompanying you?"

"Well, yeah." I look at him, my brow furrowing in confusion. It's almost like he's surprised I befriended the quiet, genteel girl. "Even if she wasn't the only one who's talking to me around here, she's my friend. I think I deserve at least one of those if I'm going to stay sane while I'm down here."

"But she is your maidservant." He still seems genuinely bewildered by what I'm saying.

"And? This is the twenty-first century; even if I did consider her my maid-servant, it's basic human decency to be nice to the people helping you." This time I'm the one raising my eyebrows at him. "Besides, she's the only person around here who seems genuinely interested in my well-being. Why wouldn't I want to be friends with her?"

Hades stiffens, his midnight-blue eyes narrowing at the edges. When he speaks, his tone is clipped, as razor-sharp as an icicle. "Again, I apologise for the situation you have been inadvertently placed in."

"It's not your fault. I understand that you have a role to fulfil." I respond lightly, leaning against the doorframe. "Hades, not to be rude, but why exactly are you here?"

"To apologise for my lack of appearance. I am not being a gracious host, so I am here to make up for that."

"Okay." I eye him suspiciously. "What exactly does the god of the Under-world consider an apology?"

"That depends on you."

"On me?" I raise an eyebrow. "Whyy?"

"I will admit that I am not as... educated as most in social etiquette." Hades says. I'm surprised to see remorse flicker through his expression for a moment. "So I propose that you suggest something. Consider it an apology in the form of a small favour."

I bite back a laugh. "Do you always speak like that?"

"How exactly?"

"Like this." I deepen my voice, raising my eyebrows at him. "With big fanciful words, like you're from the Victorian era. Do you walk around with a top hat and a cigar too?"

"I do not speak like that."

"'I do not speak like that'." I mimic, this time in a much higher pitch.

"I also do not sound like that."

"Hey, if you say so. You're the all powerful, smite-on-a-whim, ruler of the dead. I don't want to get on your bad side." I hold my hands up in the air, grinning when he gives me a look.

"You are avoiding the question."

"Okay, okay, fine. A favour." I hum slightly to myself as I pretend to think. "Oh, I know! Could you show me how the Underworld works? I've always been curious."

"I have already explained to you how it works." Hades points out, looking amused. "Why would you want me to tell you again?"

I smile and roll my eyes. "Alright, I can see you're missing the subtext here. I'll clarify. Show me your land, oh-impassive-and-almighty ruler."

"You want to see the Underworld?" Whatever amusement that had been dusting his expression vanishes, smoothly replaced with hardy solemnity. "Are you sure about that? It will not be what you expect."

"I'm expecting a land full of dead people. I'm pretty sure nothing can exceed those expectations. Unless you're trying to tell me that there are live people down here too." I joke, but his expression doesn't change. I falter. Okay. Guess the God of the Underworld doesn't like jokes. "I'm sorry. I take that back; we don't have to see the Underworld. Can we go see Cerberus instead? I've always wanted to know what he looks like."

"That, I will gladly do." Hades inclines his head, offering me his arm. "Take my arm and close your eyes. It will be much less of a discomfort if you do."

"What will?" I ask, eying him warily. He watches me with an expectant gaze, his arm hovering in the air between us. I hesitate for a moment longer before timidly placing my palm on his proffered arm, letting my eyes flutter shut.

As soon as I've closed my eyes, I hear Hades click his fingers. A sharp twisting sensation explodes in my gut, as my insides are suddenly pulled through space by my belly button. Less than two seconds later the sensation abruptly stops, and my feet smack into the ground as I crash-land into something. I press my lips together and swallow hard, my stomach churning like a washing machine. Only once my stomach stops roiling do I slowly creak my eyes open again. My jaw drops.

"We've moved." I gasp, my eyes bugging out of their sockets. "How did we move?"

"It is one of my many talents." Hades replies, his eyes twinkling. "I also retain the ability to do this."

He disappears.

"Okay." I laugh awkwardly, twirling around in a circle. "The King of the Underworld is showing off to me, right here, right now."

"I am not showing off." He suddenly speaks up from behind me. I jump so high I'm surprised I don't start orbiting around in space. Chuckling, Hades blinks back into my vision. I gawk at him.

"How do you do that?!"

"The Underworld is my realm, just as the surface is Zeus' and the ocean Poseidon's."

My nose crinkles up in confusion. "What does that mean?"

"I have the ability to manipulate the formation of the Underworld in whatever way I wish." Hades explains. "That includes being able to manipulate the air particles around me in order to make it look like I disappeared."

"In any way you want?" I raise my eyebrows at him. "So what, you could just wish for a big-ass volcano to appear and boom! The Underworld has its very own Vesuvius?"

Hades shakes his head. "Not quite. I am only able to manipulate the realm to a point. Even powerful divinities such as myself have their limits. The only ones who would be able to mould the world to that extent would be my parents."

"Rhea and Kronos?"

He nods his head once. "There is a reason they are barely mentioned in ancient mythology."

"Well... That's not a spine-chilling thought. At all." I reply sarcastically, prompting the corners of his mouth to twist up ever-so-slightly. "So exactly how does it work, then? The whole realm-manipulation-invisibility thing?"

"It is not something the human mind can grasp easily, Evie Autumn."

His impassive dismissal riles up my competitive streak. My gaze narrows.

"Try me."

"It is a matter of the mind." He replies simply, chuckling at the bewilderment that crosses my expression. Pushing open a door, Hades steps to the side and gestures me forward into a bright and blinding white light. The moment my surroundings sharpen into focus, my eyes widen in amazement. We're standing in the last place I'd expect to find in the Underworld: a beautiful, flowering, pristine garden. Rich green grass extends as far as the eye can see, with a rainbow of vibrant wildflowers peppering the ground like bright snowflakes. To my left is a sprawling, flourishing vegetable and herb garden, and to my right is the archway entrance to what looks like a gigantic rose garden. And at the very end of the garden, under the shade of a drooping willow tree, is a gargantuan wooden doghouse that casts a long shadow across a small neighbouring hut. "Just as my mode of transportation is."

"But," I wrinkle up my nose, trying not to sound stupid. "When you moved us just now, you clicked your fingers."

"I did." He acknowledges. "But only for your benefit. I can easily move us without needing to click my fingers, but I thought you would prefer a signal before I transported us through space. Others have not taken so lightly to it."

"Right." I nod slowly, trying to take it all in. "Tell me, does anything normal happen down here?"

"You are in the Underworld, Evie. Were you truly expecting normalcy?"

"Ha ha." I jokingly narrow my eyes at him. "So where exactly have you brought me, your majesty? The Fields of Punishment?"

"Why would I take you to the Fields of Punishment?" He arches an eyebrow at me. "I have brought you to Cerberus' headquarters. You said you wanted to see Cerberus."

"I know that." I laugh, shaking my head. "I'm being sarcastic, Hades. Please tell me you know what sarcasm is."

"Of course I know what sarcasm is. I invented sarcasm." He replies seriously. My jaw drops.

"I'm sorry, what?"

With a small smirk, Hades turns and whistles a sharp, singular note. For a few beats, nothing happens. Then, a low rumble starts to shake the air around me, like an earthquake gearing up to rip the ground away. I peer around Hades, just in time to see a large, black blur barreling towards us like a bullet train. I squeak, my eyes bulging out of their sockets.

"Oh my god!"

Chapter Six

Chapter Six

The barreling shadow of doom screeches to a halt before Hades and I, towering over the two of us like a skyscraper. I squeak a second time, ducking behind Hades. He laughs — actual, full-bodied chuckles— at my reaction, and steps forward to greet the big black dog.

"This is Cerberus." He scratches the dog's head, turning to me. My eyes just about bug out of my head at the sight of the two standing side by side; the top of Cerberus' shoulder is almost level with Hades' head. The monstrous dog has to crouch down just so his head is within Hades' reach.

"I can see that. Why does he look so..." I struggle to find the right words. "Semi-normal? Normal and un-normal? Normal-ish?"

"What are you surprised by?"

"Well..." I fold my arms and unfold them again, tucking my hair behind my ear as I regard them with an incredibly wary gaze. My questions bubble up through my lips before I can stop them. "Why is he so small? Why does he look like a Newfoundland? Why does he have one head?"

Hades chuckles. "He prefers to take this form when he is around those he is not familiar with. He finds that it does not scare them as much."

"You're talking about him like he's extremely intelligent." I say slowly, tentatively holding my hand out to the dog. Cerberus blinks at me, almost like he's sizing me up, and steps forward. It takes all my strength not to flinch as he draws closer. "Is he?"

"Of course." Hades replies, watching Cerberus sniff my hand. "He has the essential job of ensuring that the dead are unable to escape, and that those who do not belong in this realm do not succeed in breaching it. That task requires some degree of intelligence, would you not agree?"

"I guess." I smile and reach up on my tip-toes to scratch behind Cerberus' ears. "But that still doesn't explain why he's so small, and... well... normal." Cerberus growls softly, and I wince. "Sorry."

"He manipulates the way you perceive him; that is why you only see his smaller form. I see something quite different to you." Hades explains. "He only takes his true form when he's either guarding his post, or around myself or Aeacus. It takes him a long time to trust you enough to let you see his true form."

"You or Aeacus? What's so special about Aeacus?"

"Aeacus and Cerberus formed a... special bond, when he turned up." Hades' lips turn up ever so slightly when Cerberus' eyes light up at the sound of Aeacus' name. "Aeacus is somewhat of a recluse, and prefers to call himself Cerberus' caretaker over an official Judge of the Underworld. He will help out when he is needed, but tends to prefer the company of Cerberus over anybody else."

"That makes sense. Who wouldn't prefer his company?" I glance up at Hades and smile. "He's gorgeous."

Cerberus chuffs, almost appearing to smirk at my praise.

"I am sure he appreciates that compliment." Hades responds with a hint of amusement. He whistles again, this time two short sharp blasts, and flicks his wrist at Cerberus. "But unfortunately, he will not be remaining to hear any more. He has a rather important job to attend to."

"I understand." I nod. I pat his head one more time and bow my head. "It was an honour meeting you, Cerberus."

Cerberus barks once and licks my entire arm, causing me to erupt into giggles. After meeting his master's gaze for a moment, the majestic dog nods his head and leaps off into the darkness, disappearing as quickly as he appeared.

Hades looks back at me. The giggles die down in my throat when I realise his expression has retained its sombre seriousness once again. "I have something to show you."

"What is it?" I ask curiously, drying my arm off on my black jeans. His only response is to offer up his arm for me again. I cautiously reach forward. Without warning, I feel that same strange pulling sensation in my belly button again, and before I can properly close my eyes, my vision tunnels into darkness.

After a few seconds, my feet touch solid ground again and my vision is abruptly returned in a blinding flood of light. Hades continues forward like nothing out of the ordinary has happened. I, on the other hand, stumble forward with a gasp, my hands wildly searching for something steady as my body continues to ripple like it's still moving through space.

"Oh my—" I lean heavily on my knees, cutting myself off with a spluttering cough. "I am never going to get used to that."

Hades pauses and glances over his shoulder at me. His midnight-blue eyes widen a fraction.

"You did not close your eyes, did you?" He asks, reaching out to steady me. I shake my head, pressing my lips together into a thin, white line. "You must close your eyes when I transport us, Evie. You will feel nauseating episodes of dislocation if you attempt to witness the process."

My sardonic reply hisses out through my teeth. "Yeah, you think?"

"Are you alright?"

"Asking that is just inviting an even more sarcastic retort." I laugh breathlessly. Using his proffered arm as a support, I slowly unfold myself from my upright foetal position and breathe in deeply. "Here's an idea: why don't you just never zip zap me around like that again?"

"It is my main method of moving around the Underworld." Hades responds, moving away the moment he's sure I'm steady on my own feet. "So unless you are wanting to be left behind when we travel around the Underworld, I do not think you will find satisfaction in my answer to that question."

"Can't you just... take the bus?"

"There are no buses. Oddly enough, I am the only one who feels the need to move around the Underworld." Hades replies amusedly. Then his expression switches to one of serious sincerity, so quickly that I almost get emotional whiplash. "Your family is just around the corner in their Elysium, Evie. Are you ready to see them?"

"Wait, what?" I blink rapidly, bewildered by the sudden change of subject. His words sink in. The air around us freezes. "You—you brought me to see my family?"

"Yes. I said that I would, and I do not forgo my promises." Hades replies. He watches me with what almost looks like a touch of sympathy. "Have you changed your mind?"

"No, I just—" My throat closes up. I have to shrug several times before I'm able to get the words out. "I just didn't realise I would see them today."

"I apologise. Had I known you were expecting a warning, I would have told you. I thought it would be a pleasant surprise."

"No, don't apologise. It is a nice surprise." I offer him a small smile. "Thank you, Hades. I'd love to see them."

"Very well." Hades inclines his head and waves his hand. Suddenly, I'm not looking out into hazy darkness anymore, but at a vintage, wooden country house, equipped both with the generic white picket fence and a front porch dressed in light grey. Light dances across the white house in broken shadows, from a source up above that disappears when I look at it, and there's an all-too-familiar willow tree enveloping the front yard. Achingly familiar laughter pours out of the open front door, and more than once I see a shadow flit past the rustic windows. A golf ball lodges in my throat.

"I recognise this house. This is the house that I lived in before..." I clear my throat, shaking my head. "Why can I see this house?"

"It is your parent's Elysium. This is the house they imagined they would have lived in for the duration of their lives, had they been given the chance."

"But I thought you said that a person's Elysium depended on what they thought they deserved?"

"That is correct." Hades nods. "But it does not work as simply as that. If it did, a lot of unworthy people would receive a happy ending, when in reality what they deserve is the complete opposite. As the God of the Underworld, it is my duty to have the final say in the ultimate determination of a person's Elysium, to ensure that each and every Elysium is fairly distributed, by my judges, in accordance with that person's life. Your parents believed they deserved happiness after death; we agreed with them. This was the result."

"Oh. And that's the same for everyone then? You've determined the Elysium of every person who's ever died depending on what you think is fair?" I ask. He nods. "You've never once been tempted to sentence someone to, I don't know, eternal hell just because you don't like them?"

"Of course not." He replies seriously. "It may not seem it, Evie, but I am a very reasonable person when it comes to determining a person's Elysium. I only sentence people to eternal hell if I think they truly deserve it."

"Wait, eternal hell actually exists? You're not joking with me, are you?" I ask incredulously. His eyes merely twinkle in reply. I narrow my own eyes at him. "Stop it. You're freaking me out."

"Stop what?" He asks, somehow managing to look completely innocent. "I do not understand your request."

I burst out laughing.

"You sound like a rehearsed robot." I chuckle, rolling my eyes good-naturedly. "Do you even feel emotions?"

Hades stiffens. His expression smooths over. "Yes."

"Oh." I blink, taken aback by the iciness emanating from his tone. Nice one, me. "I'm sorry, I didn't mean to offend you. I was only joking."

Hades doesn't respond, his expression more impassive than a looming cliff-face. I half expect my limbs to stiffen into crystalline ice under his frigid gaze.

Clearing my throat, I tuck my arms under my armpits and step forward. "Can I meet them?"

"No. You cannot go any closer." He responds blankly. "This is their Elysium. Disrupting it would have dire repercussions for both your parents and yourself — repercussions that I do not have the time to regulate."

"Oh." I swallow and rock back on my feet. "Is there any way I can see them, then?"

I feel the prick of his gaze on my back as he watches me. Finally, he steps into my peripheral vision and nods tightly. "You will need to come closer. I can cloak us both with invisibility so you can see them for a few minutes, but I will only hold it for a brief period of time. After that, we must go."

"Okay." I shoot him a small smile. "Thank you, Hades."

Hades nods again and beckons me closer. Stepping forward, I cautiously place my palm on his forearm and close my eyes, well aware of what happened the last time I forgot that one small detail. Only this time, when he clicks his fingers, I'm just engulfed by an odd feeling of displacement. I open my eyes to see that the air around Hades and I now shimmers slightly at the edges. Hades glances down at me briefly, arching an eyebrow. I nod in response. He waves his hand to the side, and the next thing I know, I'm standing in the middle of a kitchen I know like the back of my hand, facing two people that I haven't seen in years. My heart stops.

It's my parents.

They haven't changed one bit since I last saw them; my mother, with her light ginger hair dusted with the first signs of ageing, and my father, with his dirty blonde hair and crow's feet in the corners of his eyes from laughing too much. They're both standing at the sink, washing dishes side-by-side and laughing between themselves at a joke my father made. The clinking of the dishes muffles the crackling of a fire in the background, and my parents' laughter breaks up the otherwise unusual silence of the house. For several moments, I strain my ears trying to figure out exactly what it is that's missing. Then my mother calls out, and I realise with a jolt what it is.

"Evie! Ellie! Dessert's almost ready! Can you please come and set the table?"

My eyes widen. I take a couple of steps forward just in time to see two strawberry-blonde girls rush into the room, giggling and pushing each other in their haste to beat their rival to the table. You only need to take one cursory look at them to know that they're identical twins; it was only those who were really close to the twins that could really tell them apart. The easiest way was, of course, their eyes: one had eyes the colour of the deepest rivers, and the other eyes the colour of the ocean.

It takes me several tries to clear my throat enough to get a full sentence out. When I finally succeed, my voice is hoarse. "Is that...?"

"You and your sister?" He finishes my sentence. I nod. "Yes, it is. Your family's conception of Elysium is that of utter happiness, which included you at the age that they all died. For all they know, you died alongside them."

Wrapping my arms around myself tightly, I watch my family move around my childhood home in complete silence, unable to tear my attention away from them. My throat closes up. The more time that passes, the more I find myself desperately missing it; missing the comfort of the family that was torn so callously away from me. I'd almost forgotten how much I missed them, or how empty Hades' palace had felt without my new family until now.

"Why me?" I finally ask, my voice softer than a whisper. Hades looks at me quizzically. "Why did Spencer and my... foster family choose me?"

"That is not of relevant importance."

I still. "What?"

"It is a factor you do not need to know."

"I understood you the first time Hades. You mean you know?" I ask. He nods once. I clear my throat several times, crossing my arms over my chest as I attempt to process it all. "So you're telling me, you know exactly why I was raised for the last ten years by Greek gods, but you're going to keep it a secret from me because it's 'not of relevant importance'?"

"Yes."

"Seriously?" I can't help but laugh, his apathetic words rendering me in shock. My annoyance twists my words into bitterly-spoken barbs. "What gives you that right? This is my life we are talking about, and you're purposefully keeping me in the dark about half of it. How on earth is that fair?"

"I apologise, Evie. I did not mean to upset you with this." Hades tells me impassively. "That was not my intention."

"You're not answering my question." I retort. My attention is now completely stolen from my family as I face him head-on. The moment I give Hades my full attention the house slowly fades away into the background, softening at the edges until it has disappeared altogether. "Why are you keeping this a secret from me, Hades?"

Hades hesitates, only for a fraction second, but it's long enough for me to catch the guilt that flashes through his eyes. Then it's gone, and his expression is blank once more. "That is also something I cannot tell you."

I blink at him rapidly. "You can't tell me? You trick me into agreeing to a deal that was practically made null-and-void by the fact that the person I was saving is a god, then say in the same breath that I was raised for the last ten year by a bunch of gods, and now you suddenly know exactly why that is, but you can't tell me?"

"That is correct."

I swallow and nod several times. I'm so overwhelmed by shock that I physically feel sick. Clearing my throat, I take a step back, throwing up sky-high walls between us in the same action. "I'd like to go back to my room. Now, please."

Hades' jaw clenches. He nods tightly. "Very well."

He clicks his fingers. With a crippling wave of nausea that hits me like a bullet train, everything twists into overwhelming darkness, and Hades disappears.

— — —

"Evie?!"

I open my eyes with a gasp, stumbling against a wall as another wave of nausea punches me in the gut. Once the feeling recedes, I slide down the wall, bending my head forward and pressing every part of my body against the cool marble floor. I slowly suck in a ragged breath. Now I understood why Hades insisted I hold onto him when he transported us around — it feels like I left eighty percent of my insides behind.

"Evie?" Someone tentatively touches my shoulder. I jump about a mile in the air, wildly looking up. Disappointment surges through me.

It's Calla.

"Oh. Hi." I swallow and smile tightly at her. "Don't mind me. I'm just gonna sit here for a few minutes and try not to throw up the majority of my internal organs."

"Why?" She offers me a hand up.

I smile at her gratefully and pull myself up, making a face when my stomach heaves. "Let's just say I discovered why Hades prefers to escort people around instead of zapping them places."

"Why was he zapping you places?"

I grimace. "I may or may not have let my temper get the better of me, which made him mad, so..."

"So he zapped you to your room." She finishes, helping me over to my bed. "Why are you angry with him?"

I sigh, drawing my knees up to my chest.

"Hades told me that he, along with apparently every single person I know, is keeping a secret from me. A secret that I'm ninety percent sure is the reason my foster family was the divine version of the Brady Bunch. And when I tried to ask him about it, he, well..." I gesture towards myself, throwing my hands up in the air with a humourless laugh. "So, yeah. For someone who personally hates people keeping secrets from her... there's that."

Calla flinches at the bitterness clouding my tone. "What do you mean, every single person you know? I'm not keeping secrets from you."

"No. You're right. You're not." I twist my lips to the side and shoot her a small smile. "I'm sorry Calla. I shouldn't be taking my frustration out on you. That's not fair."

"It's okay." She smiles at me and pats my hand. We sit in awkward silence for a few minutes before she tentatively speaks up again. "I get the feeling that is not the only reason you're frustrated. Is there something else bothering you, Miss Evie?"

I fall back on my bed and blow my cheeks out. "Not something."

"Someone?" She guesses. I hold a thumb up in the air. "Hades?"

"Who else?" I snort.

"Why is he bothering you?"

"It's not him, per se, it's just that..." I hesitate, chewing on the inside of my cheek. "I'm suddenly unsure as to whether this was a good decision or not."

"What decision?"

"The decision to stay here. In the Underworld. To honour my deal with Hades." I prop myself up on my elbows and look at her.

"Why are you unsure about that?"

"I guess a part of me always thought I would actually be able to do this, even when Hades disappeared for the first few weeks." I shrug. "Even after the dinner on my first night here, where I found out about the whole every-single-person-in-my-life-being-a-Greek-god situation, I thought I could at least trust Hades — which sounds weird, I know, but he seemed genuine, and at the time I thought he was the only one who hadn't lied to me."

"Alright." Calla nods slowly as she processes it all. "I sense a 'but' coming up."

"Your senses are not wrong." I sigh. "After what Hades told me, or didn't tell me, I don't feel as confident about being able to keep my promise anymore."

"Why?"

"Because I hate people keeping secrets from me. I hate it. I feel like I can't trust someone when I know they've been lying to me, especially if they're lying about something that'll affect me. And now that I know that Hades has been keeping something from me this whole time, something big, I don't know if I can trust him. I don't know who I can trust anymore."

Calla's quiet for a second. "You can trust me."

"That's true. I can." Her comment draws a small smile out of me. I reach over and squeeze her hand. "And I do. So thank you."

Calla smiles for a moment, but then she hesitates, her expression wavering as several emotions visibly battle for control. She abruptly stands up, sending a shuddering jolt through the entire bed, and moves away to frantically fluff up the cushions on my sofa. Her head remains firmly bowed as she mumbles something under her breath.

"You're better than her."

"What?" My forehead crinkles in confusion. "Better than who?"

The pillow drops from Calla's hands. She blanches. "N-nothing. I didn't say anything."

"Calla, I know you just said something. I heard you." I frown at her. "Please don't start lying to me now; you just said I could trust you. You just said that you weren't keeping secrets from me."

"Yes. I'm not keeping secrets from you." She stammers, shifting on the spot. Her eyes dart around the room, her behaviour growing flightier the more I stare her down.

"So why are you suddenly unable to look me in the eye?" I persist, sliding off the bed and crossing my arms over my chest. When she still doesn't say anything, I start rapidly firing off questions at her like bullets. She flinches every time one leaves my lips. "Who are you talking about? Why can't you tell me about her? What are you keeping from me? Are you in on it too? Have you been lying to me too?"

Calla bites her lip, blanching so much that her dark skin lightens several shades. "I'm really not supposed to say..."

"Calla, please. Please tell me." I beg. "I don't want to spend my four months here in a web of secrets and lies, not knowing who I can trust."

"That's a bit of an exaggeration." She says. Her eyes flicker to the door. It remains fastidiously fastened shut. She licks her lips several times and steps closer to me. Her voice lowers. "Do you know why you're here, Miss Autumn?"

"To repay my debt." I speak slowly. "Why?"

"Because that is not why you are really here. It is just a farce." She steps even closer, twisting her fingers. Her voice barely registers at a whisper. "You're here because—"

A sharp rap sounds at the door. Calla stops, the blood draining from her face. Breaking eye contact with me, she darts over to the door and pulls it open to reveal Hades. Calla squeaks and scurries from the room, flinching as she passes Hades.

Inwardly, I groan. She was so close to telling me the truth. But now, judging from the pure, unadulterated fear that had flashed across her face when she neared Hades, I'll probably be lucky if she even looks at me.

So close.

I fold my arms and regard Hades with a steely expression. "Can I help you?"

Hades silently watches Calla go, shutting the door quietly behind her. He regards me with a cool gaze, his expression smoother than a lake before a storm, but doesn't respond. I try again after a few more beats of silence.

"What do you want, Hades? I'm not particularly in the mood to speak to you. In fact, I'm feeling slightly queasy at the thought."

"I am sorry." He says quietly. "I acted out of anger. For that, I apologise."

"Thank you." I reply tightly, turning away. " You can see yourself out."

"Evie." His low melodious voice stops me in my tracks. "That is not all I am sorry for."

I pause, and turn my head. "What else are you sorry for?"

Hades exhales, sounding unusually irresolute.

"For what happened earlier." He tells me. I'm rewarded with a rare sighting of remorse on his features. "I know I said that I would not keep any secrets from you, and I have already done that. But you must trust that I am only trying to make things as pleasant as they can be for you, not upset you."

"Then why are you keeping secrets from me?" I ask. "Why am I really here, Hades? And don't tell me it's because of the deal we made, because you and I both know that's bull."

"There are some things that simply cannot be explained at this moment, Evie." He replies, looking apologetic. "You just need to trust me when I say that I would tell you if I could."

I sigh, chewing on the inside of my cheek. A large part of me doesn't want to believe him, but the sincerity on his face is genuine. And after weeks of looking at a blank slate, I just know that he's telling the truth for once.

"Okay." I say quietly. "I understand."

"Thank you, Evie." Hades inclines his head and steps forward. It's only then that I notice his hands are behind his back.

I eye him suspiciously. "What are you hiding behind your back?"

"A gift."

My eyebrows shoot up. "A gift? For what?"

"For you." His reply has me choking back a laugh. "That is a traditional custom mortals partake in when they want to apologise, correct? Offer up gifts as peace offerings?"

I glance down at my fingers, grinning. "Sometimes."

"This must be one of those times then." A small smile ghosts across his lips, and he brings something out from behind his back.

My eyes widen. I cover my mouth with my hand, laughing in disbelief. "Oh, you can't be serious."

"I am always serious." He tells me, his eyes twinkling like the night sky.

I can't stop the delight from lighting up my face. I squeal, reaching forward eagerly. "He's adorable!"

Hades chuckles quietly and places the small black kitten in my arms. It mewls softly, melting me on the spot with its magnetic sapphire-blue eyes.

"He is yours, if you want him. I understand how lonely it can get down here, and having a companion can assist in preventing that."

"But how is it possible he's here at all?" I gasp when a horrific thought strikes me. "He's not... dead, is he?"

"Of course not. He is unique, like Cerberus."

"What do you mean, unique?"

"Have you heard of the Nemean Lion?"

"Yes." My eyes narrow sceptically. "What are you saying, Hades?"

"This is one of the lion's less famous siblings." Hades informs me. "He is immortal, of course, and Aeacus will assist you in looking after him when he grows. He will have his own quarters like Cerberus in due time, but for now he is under your care."

"Oh, absolutely not." I scoff. Hades quirks an eyebrow at me. "He's sleeping in my room, no matter what. I don't care how big he gets."

Hades actually laughs at that. I can't help but smile at the warm, melodic sound.

"Thank you, Hades."

"You do not need to thank me." He smiles back at me. "This is my way of apologising to you for my behaviour."

"But you've already apologised."

"I know." He answers, watching the kitten in my hands. "But I just want to ensure you are aware that I truly am sorry. I would tell you if I could."

"I know." I shoot him a reassuring smile. "I just wanted an explanation. And I got one... kind of."

"Very well." Hades inclines his head, moving towards the door. He looks over his shoulder at me, pausing with his hand on the frame. "I hope, in time, you will find it in yourself to trust me, Evie."

Then he leaves, the door quietly clicking into place behind him.

I watch him go, still holding the squirming kitten in my arms. Pursing my lips, I slowly sit down on my bed and let the kitten fall down onto my lap. He sneezes and paws at my knees, looking up at me with a mewl. I grin and obediently stroke him. A laugh bubbles up over my lips when he starts purring.

"You know, he is probably the most confusing person I've ever met in my life." I tell the kitten quietly. "And that's saying something; my best friend is Spencer."

The kitten sneezes again, almost like he's agreeing with me, and head-butts my knee. I chuckle softly, shaking my head.

"Well, hey. At least I got something good out of his confusing personality." I scratch his ears. My gaze flickers back up to the door, and I smile. "Maybe this won't be so bad after all."

Chapter Seven

C hapter Seven

Later that day, I'm in my room, completely enraptured watching my new kitten chase his own tail, when I hear a loud knock. I blink, staring at the door in confusion. Calla hadn't returned since she fled from Hades this morning, and I knew for a fact that it definitely wasn't Hades; expecting two visits in one day from him was just laughable.

The person knocks again, jolting me out of my reverie. I jump and push myself up to my feet, crossing over to the door. Placing my hand on the doorknob, I lean in and hesitantly call out.

"Hello?"

An unfamiliarly nasal voice responds. "Yes, hello. I have your room service here."

"Room service?" I frown and swing open the door. "I didn't order any room service—"

The sentence dies in my throat. The person standing in front of me let out a triumphant exclamation, their voice returning to normal.

"Oh, it is the right room! I could've sworn that red-head I talked to pur-posefully tried to direct me to the fiery pits of Hell—"

"Spencer?"

Spencer grins at me, his cheeky smirk achingly familiar. "That was my name, last time I checked."

I falter, holding the door. "What are you doing here?"

"I came here for the cotton candy." He deadpans. "Why do you think I'm here?"

"The cotton candy." I throw back at him, folding my arms across my chest.

"Okay. I deserved that." He winces, running a hand through his dirty-blonde hair. "I'm sorry, E. I messed up. I know I messed up. And, look, I know you don't want to see me, but can you at least hear me out before you completely shut me out?"

I glare at him for a few more seconds. My shoulders relax. "Fine."

A relieved smile breaks out onto Spencer's face. He lets out a breathy laugh. "Thank you."

I don't respond, merely stepping to the side. Spencer ducks his head and slips past me. I shut the door and sit down on the opposite end of the bed, watching Spencer silently as he paces around my room awkwardly. He finally settles for leaning against the post of my bed and crossing his arms. The kitten, sensing my shift in mood, trots over to me and twines around my ankles, screaming at me to pick him up. Spencer's jaw just about hits the floor.

"Is that a kitten?"

"Maybe."

"What the hell is it doing here? In Hell?"

"Hades gave it to me."

Spencer scoffs. "You can't be serious."

"Yes Spencer, you're right. I'm not serious. No, instead I went into the Underworld, found a dead kitten, and snuck it into the palace before anybody noticed." I roll my eyes at him. "Yes, Hades gave it to me. Why is that such a surprise?"

Spencer cocks an eyebrow at me, staring at me.

"What?"

He shakes his head, throwing me one of his winning smiles. "Nothing. It's just... surprising, that's all."

I give him a look. "Yeah, that's a great idea Spence. Start off your apology for all the secrets you kept from me with another secret."

Spencer flinches under my withering gaze. "Alright, alright, point taken. Put away your death glare already."

I huff, returning my attention back to the kitten. Having successfully managed to claw his way up my leg during our conversation, he curls up into a small black ball next to me, tired from his intrepid climb. I smile and stroke his head with the back of my index finger.

"I think I'm going to call him Pluto."

Spencer snorts. "Oh come on, E. The Roman name for 'Hades'? Don't you think that's a little on the nose?"

"What? It fits, don't you think?"

"Oh yes, sure it does. Name the kitten after Hades; boost his ego. That'll make our lives so much better."

"What's your problem with Hades?" I ask bemusedly. "He's not that bad."

"I beg to differ. You're forgetting, Miss Autumn, that I've known him for a lot longer than you can possibly imagine." Spencer pushes himself off the bedpost, his questioning gaze flickering to the empty spot next to me. I shake my head at him, but Spencer just rolls his eyes in response and physically shoves me aside, flopping down on the bed with a loud sigh. My gaze narrows.

"You're forgetting that I didn't know that specific detail until a month ago."

He winces. "Evie..."

I pause to let him finish. When he doesn't say anything, I hold my hands up and cock an eyebrow at him. "What? Please, do explain, Spencer. I've been dying to know why you kept something as big as the fact that you're a literal Greek god from me when you, out of all people, know exactly why I hate secrets."

Spencer blows out his cheeks. For the first time in my life, he looks completely unsure of what to say. "I wish I could tell you everything Evie, but..."

"Let me guess. It's a secret that's better left a secret for the time being."

Spencer nods. "You have to understand Evie, this is much bigger than you think. Even if I wanted to, I'm not allowed to tell you everything. Zeus would smite me if I did, and I really don't enjoy it when he does that. The smell of burning hair lingers, you know."

I groan. "That's what everyone's saying, and it's starting to get ridiculously annoying. Can't anyone tell me anything?"

"I can tell you that we all do care about you." He says. I give him a look. "I'm serious, E. Even though we only met you because of Hades'... thing, we didn't realise how amazing you'd be, or how easy it would be to love you. We only half-faked the whole family vibe, I swear."

"Half-faked?"

"Well, yeah." Spencer shrugs, grinning at me. "Towards the end, I think our dysfunctional little group started to believe it really could be a family. Y'know, before Hades stepped in and had me murdered."

"Why did he? Kill you, I mean."

"That's where my inability to talk about it kicks in, unfortunately." Spencer grimaces. "I do need to talk to Hades about that, though. We had a deal that I would die in style, not like a damn dog in the street."

"Of course it is." I wrinkle up my nose in frustration and let out a long sigh. "I've officially decided that I hate all gods. You suck."

"Hey." Spencer nudges me. "I take great offence to that. How dare you associate me with that boring ol' bunch."

"You're missing the point, Spencer."

"I think it's fairly obvious the one missing the point is you, my dear mortal compatriot—" Spencer flinches when I raise a fist, holding his hands up in the air. "Okay, okay, I'm sorry. But I do still take personal offence at that 'hate all gods' comment. We're not all that bad. It's the Egyptians you really have to look out for; they're as sneaky as those felines they fangirl over."

I shake my head, somewhat exasperatedly. "I'm still struggling to comprehend the whole 'we'. I mean you, a god?"

"Oh, come now, Evie." Spencer winks cheekily at me. "Don't deny it. I know you thought I was god-like at least once or twice."

I shove him off the bed. "Could you be any more self-centred?"

He smirks up at me. "I'm a god, Evie. I don't think that's even a possibility."

I burst out laughing. He watches me with a little smile on his face, his cerulean-blue eyes twinkling.

"This is ridiculous." I giggle. "My best friend is a god. My foster-family are gods. I am living in the Underworld with a god. This whole thing is ridiculous."

"That sounds like a dilemma, that does." Spencer responds seriously. He leans against the bed with a thoughtful expression on his face. "Why on earth would you put up with all of that? It's giving you awful stress wrinkles."

"Why don't you come back up here so I can push you off the bed again?"

"Now, now, Evie. What have I said about those violent tendencies of yours?" He tuts, shaking his head. "I can look past them of course, but if you don't keep them in check, Hades won't want you around as much."

My smile vanishes. I clear my throat and pat the bed next to me. "No really, come back up. Now that you've spilled the divine beans, I want to hear all about your misguided godly adventures."

"You don't need to ask me twice." Spencer smirks. Pulling himself up, he positions himself against the plethora of pillows and links his arms behind his head. "Where shall I begin?"

"The beginning?" I reply. Spencer laughs. I stare at him. "No Spencer, I'm serious. Start at the beginning. And leave nothing out."

— — —

The next few hours pass us by in what feels like the blink of an eye. I hadn't realised until I actually saw Spencer how isolated I had truly felt, or how much I had just missed my closest friend. Yes, he'd hurt and betrayed me, but he'd been there for me since I was ten years old, and he never failed to make me smile. And it was because of that, especially in my current predicament, that I knew I'd never be able to stay truly mad at him.

"No. No. You can't be serious!" I gape at him. Over the hours, we'd slowly migrated to the floor and ended up playing a card game, of all things. "You were engaged to Cleopatra?"

"I may lie about some things Evie, but I definitely wouldn't lie about that." Spencer chuckles. "Do you have an eight?"

"No. Go fish." I retort. He grumbles and picks a card up off the pile. I shuffle forward. "So what happened?"

"I was a touch drunk in Egypt one night, and somehow found myself in the royal palace, sharing a bottle of wine with her royal highness. And then I found myself seducing her, in her bedchambers. So naturally, we got married." Spencer shrugs. "It lasted about six hours. Then I unexpectedly had to dash. She was inconsolable, understandably."

"'Unexpectedly had to dash'?" I snort. "What did you do, seduce someone else?"

"More or less." Spencer grimaces. "It would be an understatement to say dear Cleo wasn't very impressed with me when she stumbled across us. She threatened to sic a lot of native Egyptian animals on me."

"You are a disgusting, horrible little man." I shake my head. "Don't you have any sort of restraint?"

"I'm Dionysus, the patron god of wine, revelry and ecstasy. What do you think?"

A soft knock sounds at my door. We both pause, and twist around to see Calla timidly slipping in my door. She bows her head.

"Master Dionysus, Master Hermes has requested you be informed that he is ready to depart. Miss Evie, Hades requests your presence in the dining hall."

"No!" I wail childishly. Then I process what she said. I frown and look over at Spencer. "Wait, Olly's here? Why is Olly here?"

"He's the only one aside from the Big Three who can travel between the realms, so he's my only way down here." Spencer shrugs. "Besides, he had something he needed to tell Hades, apparently. Super secret messenger godly stuff, or something. It didn't take much begging and whining on my part before he agreed to let me tag along."

"Oh. Right." I glance back at Calla and smile at her sheepishly. "Do I have to go? I've been having so much fun playing cards and tearing down Spencer's ego."

Spencer grunts and flicks a card at me. "Leave my ego out of this."

Calla doesn't respond to my question. Instead, her eyes widen in avid fascination as she slowly turns the card around in her hand.

"What are these?"

"They're cards." I laugh. "Wait, are you telling me you've never seen cards before?"

"No." She breathes, looking up at me with a big smile. "Can I try them?"

I glance over at Spencer. He shrugs.

"Why not? Olly can wait; this looks much more interesting."

Teaching Calla how to play cards was the most entertaining thing I'd done in a long time. She seemed to grasp the basic concept of it, but didn't fundamentally understand the basic rules; she wanted an explanation for everything. Spencer wasn't much help either; he teased and poked fun at her until even I wanted to throw things at him.

And then, for some obscure, absurd, unknown reason, we moved onto poker. Which Calla was abysmal at.

After the third consecutive round of complete poker-anhilliation, Calla finally throws her cards down, her face scrunching up in a rare tantrum.

"That's not fair! I don't understand how you can tell!"

I fight back a smile, patting her on the arm. "When you're bluffing Calla, you have to keep a straight face, or we can kind of tell that you're bluffing. That's the whole point of poker."

"Or, on the other hand, you could keep playing the way that you do. It makes the game so much more fun." Spencer offers with an impish grin.

"That's not helping!"

"Helping people was never in my job description." He pushes himself up to a stand, stretching his back out. "Pissing people off, now that's much more in my wheelhouse. I've done a number on Olly; I think he's clear ready to kill me after that extra round of poker. The carpet outside your bedroom is certainly wearing it."

"I did warn you; suggesting he 'make all buddy-buddy with Satan' was only going to get you so far." I roll my eyes good-naturedly. "Do you really have to go?"

"I'd love to stay. Really, I would." He tells me with a small grimace. "Unfortunately though, I'm not able to stay in the Underworld for very long without becoming extremely, violently ill. One of the downsides of being one of the gods not technically allowed down under for an extended amount of time."

"Yet you stayed for the whole afternoon?"

Spencer offers me a hand, pulling me to a stand. He winks. "Anything for you, gorgeous."

I narrow my eyes. "I may have forgiven you a little for what you did, but sweet talking me will get you nowhere fast, Spencer."

Spencer winces. He scratches the side of his head sheepishly. "Fair point. And I will make it up to you Evie, I promise. But right now, I must bid you adieu, for I fear I might implode, and that would look horrible with the decorations in here."

I chuckle, trying to keep my voice light. "You're the biggest drama king I know."

"Yes, well, just you wait until you really meet Hades." He mutters, shooting me a short smile. "I'll be back soon, yeah?"

"Sure you will. Make sure you say hi to Olly for me, will you?" I grin, playfully punching his shoulder. He cringes, his face twisting up in pain. Alarm fizzles through me. I shove him towards the door. "Go, Spencer! You're hurting more than you're letting on, aren't you?"

"Of course he is; he's a god. They all have their own form of a 'show-no-pain complex'." Calla mumbles. She ducks her head with a blush when we turn to stare at her.

"Keep this one close, Evie. She'll keep you sane in this hellhole." Spencer grins, pointing his finger at her. Then he bows, twirls on his heel, and disappears from sight.

Calla huffs, rolling her eyes. "He's always been such a drama king."

I stare at the spot he had just been standing in. "How did he do that?"

"Show off, you mean? I'm sure it comes naturally to him."

I hold back a laugh when I see her face. "You really don't like him, do you?"

"I am not overly fond of him, no."

"Why?"

"I have my reasons." Calla replies shortly. She blanches when she sees the look on my face, and abruptly changes the subject. "Can you teach me another card game?"

I furrow my eyebrows at her, a frown worming its way onto my lips. Despite their reassurances that it was for my 'own good,' and I would find out 'in time', everyone was still being so frustratingly secretive — even Spencer. And the more information I uncovered, the more confusing things got. The more confusing things got, the more they centred around one person: Hades. And the more frustrated I got.

What was going on?

"Evie?" Calla taps my arm. I blink and turn to her, tilting my head questioningly. Her face is brightened with innocent eagerness as she repeats her earlier. "Can you teach me another card game?"

"Yes, Evie." Another voice pipes up from right behind me. I yelp and whirl around, to find Hades watching me with impassive blue eyes, his expression as blank as ever. "Will you teach us another game?"

Chapter Eight

Chapter Eight

Calla squeaks and flees from the room. I sigh and turn around.

"Can you stop doing that? You're going to give her a heart attack."

The corners of Hades' eyes crease. "Calla is already dead, Evie. She cannot have a heart attack."

"That's not the point I'm trying to make!" I splutter, throwing a card in his direction. Hades catches it without moving a muscle. I glower at him.

"What is the point you are attempting to make?" He places the card down on the bed next to him.

"Stop zip-zapping everywhere and scaring my friend! And stop being so casual about it all!" I toss another card at him. I feel an odd sense of satisfaction when it hits him square in the face.

"Would you stop throwing cards at me?"

"Maybe." I huff over-dramatically. "Would you stop keeping secrets?"

The smile drops so quickly from Hades' face you'd think I'd slapped him. His tone turns icy.

"No. I cannot."

I falter, taking a step back. "I'm sorry. I was only joking around. I know you can't."

Hades' expression doesn't lighten at my apology. "Never bring it up, not even in jest. You may not believe me, but I do not enjoy keeping secrets. Particularly from you."

Inwardly, I sigh. But outwardly, I nod.

"Okay." His eyebrow raises slightly, and I shrug. "I mean it. Okay. I trust that you'll tell me. Eventually."

"Why?" Hades asks, his voice soft. He elaborates when he catches the look of confusion twisting my face up. "Why do you trust me?"

"I don't know; you asked me to?" My nose crinkles up in confusion. Hades tilts his head to the side questioningly, so I pause as I think. "I know that we're only just getting to know each other, and that we hadn't really met before Spencer 'died,' but I feel like I've known you my whole life. You feel familiar. And for some strange reason, I trust you completely."

Hades doesn't respond; he just watches me with an unreadable expression. I gingerly sit down on the edge of my bed, leaning back against the bedpost.

"Why are you looking at me like that?"

"No reason." He says mildly. In a blink he's standing in front of me, shuffling a pack of cards. "So, how good do you think you are at poker?"

I can't stop the self-assured smirk that spreads across my lips. "I'm alright. I was taught by Spencer, after all."

"Very well then." He clicks his fingers, and a table and chair appear in front of us. Hades sits down, his eyes sparkling. "If you truly believe yourself to be that good, then I'm sure you would not mind playing me for a few rounds."

"Play you?" I blink, taken aback. "You want to play me at poker? For what, money?"

"Well, I am sure that we can find a more interesting currency if that is what you wish." Hades shuffles the cards so quickly between his hands that they become a blue blur. He arches an eyebrow at me. "Unless, of course, your hesitation is your humble way of admitting defeat?"

"Are you, Hades, Lord of the Underworld, baiting me?" I scoff and narrow my eyes. He doesn't respond, his eyebrow only arching higher. "Oh, you're on. We will play poker, but only if I get to decide the currency."

"Very well. What do you suggest we use as currency?"

"Secrets." I propose, without hesitation. His brows furrow slightly, so I elaborate. "Every time we lose, we have to answer a question the other person—"

"I accept." Hades interrupts, placing the cards on the table with a crisp snap. He looks up and motions to the chair in front of me. "Shall we begin?"

— — —

"Okay, that's it." I cross my arms childishly and scowl at him. "How are you doing this? You can't be that good at poker!"

It takes me an embarrassingly long time to realise that I'd stupidly agreed to play poker with Hades. I don't know how he did it, but he had some sort of uncanny knack of knowing exactly when I was bluffing. Every. Single.

Time. Which meant that I ended up revealing a lot more to him than I intended; more than I had ever revealed to anyone — even Spencer.

The first round we played, I lost. So he found out about my tattoo; an orchid on my ankle, my sister's favourite flower.

The second round I lost as well. So he found out about the time that I nearly drowned in the ocean when I was six. That was a secret that seemed to genuinely shock him — which I didn't think was even possible.

I also lost the third, fourth, six, seventh, ninth and tenth rounds. So Hades found out about the pet hamster I accidentally killed by burying alive (how was I to know hamsters hibernated at that age?), my relationship count (which was, sadly, still at 0), why I never wear socks (it's not my fault my feet feel too claustrophobic) and several other cheek-burning secrets.

He revealed two secrets. Two.

One — he was a big dog person (big surprise there). And two — he hated losing (at least we had that in common).

Finally, my infuriation at the continuous butt-whooping I was receiving finally manages to take the reins, resulting in me throwing my cards down and huffing loudly.

Hades raises an eyebrow at my outburst, placing his cards face-up on the table. My scowl deepens at his hand.

Well, there goes another round to him.

"What can I say? I am extremely adept at knowing when people are lying."

"Well, that's not fair!" I complain. "How can I expect to win if you've got a secret power up your sleeve? You shouldn't be allowed to use your secret powers to beat me!"

"Is winning the game not allowed now?" He chuckles, gathering up the cards and shuffling them expertly.

"Not the way you're winning. You're cheating. That's just... it's not cool."

"I am not cheating." Hades replies sincerely. I scoff. "Shall we play again, so I can prove that?"

"You can't—"

My response is cut off by a big yawn. My eyes flicker up to the clock and widen when I realise what the time is. We'd been going for nearly two and a half hours. Suddenly, I'm extremely aware of the situation I'm in. I inadvertently blush.

"Actually, it's getting pretty late..."

"Say no more." Hades stands up. As soon as he does so, the table and chair disappear, along with the cards. He slips his hands in his pockets and looks at me, his expression as unreadable as always. "I do have one last request before I leave, though."

"What is it?"

"I believe that, as I won that last round, you owe me one more secret."

"Fine." My eyes narrow good-naturedly. "What's your question?"

"Why do you hate secrets?"

His calmly-asked question floors me. My whole body freezes, as if hit by a mallet of ice. I blink at him several times, feeling the ever-familiar mask of indifference instinctively sweeping over my features. I clear my throat and lower my gaze.

"Ask me another question."

Hades gives me a quizzical look. "I'm sorry?"

"I won't answer that. Ask me another question." My tone is more forceful this time.

I feel the hot prick of his gaze on my face, but refuse to meet it. When I finally do look up, there's a singular emotion burning in his midnight-blue eyes.

Understanding.

"I will save my question for another time, then." Hades inclines his head at me. He gives me a small smile. "Good night, Evie."

With a swish from his long black trench coat, he clicks his fingers and disappears from sight.

— — —

The next morning, I sleep in for the first time since I'd arrived in the Underworld. It's not until the clock is crawling close to midday that I finally wake up, confused and bewildered as to why I'd not been woken up earlier; that's when I realise that, also for the first time since I'd arrived in the Underworld, Calla hadn't come to wake me up. I didn't even realise until that moment that I'd grown accustomed to my own little routine, and to be completely honest, that little shift threw me completely.

By the time I finally manage to get out of bed and shower, it's already well-past midday, and my stomach is growling ferociously. So, I make the executive decision to find the kitchen. The trouble was, I didn't actually know where it was. Calla had always brought me my breakfast, and I'd always found myself in a big hall for lunch; how I got there, I never really knew. But finding that hall seemed like the best place to start, so I decide to try my luck at locating it.

Even though it's such a small experience, it feels weird finally leaving my room. Obviously I'd left it before, but I was always in the company of Hades, Calla or another servant. I'd never actually left by myself — particularly since the doorknob incident all those weeks ago. I may have kicked up a fuss about it at the time, but when I was finally provided with the opportunity to leave, I didn't know what to do with myself. I was just little old me, and Hades' castle was massive. If I wasn't careful, I just knew that I'd easily get lost, and I wasn't sure I knew enough people down here to save me.

But then again, desperate times call for desperate measures, and a hungry Evie was definitely desperate Evie.

What I didn't realise until I started exploring, however, was just how massive the palace really was. I wandered down hallways and through rooms for what felt like hours, only to succeed in making myself even more lost. I discovered humongous lounges, adorned with majestic fireplaces and big velvet couches, several similarly-sized bedrooms, and my personal favourite: an enormous, majestic, bookshelf-laden library. The book nerd within me desperately wanted to stay and explore the library some more, but by that point my growling stomach had evolved into a roaring monster, so I hurried off and mentally reminded myself to ask someone for directions for next time.

Weirdly enough, though, in all my explorations I didn't come across a single person. I'd assumed that the big palace would be teeming with life, but either they were all extremely quiet, or just didn't want to see me, because I didn't encounter anyone.

So when I stumbled around a corner and saw someone walking away with what looked like a handful of dirty dishes, we can all safely assume that I sprinted after them like a starving woman would towards the buffet of her dreams.

"Hey!" I call out, panting slightly. The person pauses, turning around to reveal a young olive-skinned woman. She stares at me, her pixie-like features creased with wariness.

"Can I help you?" She asks, eyeing me up and down. I try not to shrink back under her judgmental gaze.

"No, I'm just running after you for the hell of it." I snap sarcastically. A finely styled eyebrow shoots up at my choice of words. "I'm sorry. That was rude. I'm just really hungry, and I was really hoping you might be able to lead me to the promised land."

"You're dead." The girl replies, not unkindly. "You don't need to eat. In fact, you shouldn't be here at all. How did you get past Cerberus? I should really be calling security..."

"Wait, that's it? You die and you stop needing to eat food?" I stare at her incredulously. "What kind of Elysium is this?"

The girl snorts and turns away. "You got me. Now wait here; someone will be along shortly to escort you to your Elysium."

"No please, wait!" I start after her, grabbing her arm. She freezes in her tracks. Her eyes widen as she turns to stare at me. "What? Oh I'm sorry, are you one of those personal space people?"

"You're hot." She whispers. She grabs my wrist, and her striking amethyst eyes get even wider. "And you have a pulse! How is that possible?"

"Um, genetics?" I look at her weirdly. "All living things have a pulse?"

"You're alive?" She gawks at me. "How are you here?"

I stare at her in complete confusion for several seconds. Then my mind connects the dots. "Oh, right, realm of the dead! Yes, I'm alive; I'm just staying here for four months to pay off a deal I made with Hades."

Recognition dawns on her face. If possible, she scrutinises me even harder. "You're Evie?"

"I was the last time I checked. Right now, though, I'm hungry more than anything else." I smile pleadingly. "Could you...?"

She starts, blinking several times. "Oh yes, of course! I was just heading to the kitchen anyway. Follow me."

"You're a lifesaver." I reply gratefully, hurrying after her. "Thank you."

"No problem. I'm Kezia, by the way."

"Kezia." I nod, making note of her name. "You know, I don't mean to offend you at all when I say this, but... I have to say, you're exactly the kind of person I expected to find when I first came down here."

Kezia raises her eyebrows. "What do you mean by that?"

I gesture to her black clothes, blood-red hair and heavyset eyeliner. "I don't know, more...."

"Gothic? That's extremely stereotypical of you." I flinch at the bite in her tone. She grins. "Relax, I'm kidding. This is just my most recent getup. I was getting sick of all the Victorian corsets; modern corsets are so much more comfortable."

I gape at her. "Wait, how old are you?"

"How old is the universe?" Kezia quips back. She snickers when my face scrunches up in confusion. "You might find it more beneficial to ask who I am rather than how old I am."

"Who you are?" Kezia waits in bemused silence as I visibly tick over her words. My eyes widen rapidly. "Oh! Are you saying that you're a goddess?"

"One could say that, yes." She shrugs, pushing open a door and gesturing me inside.

"Who are you then? Wait, no, let me guess!" I say eagerly, ducking my head as I walk through the doorway. Warmth smacks me in the face as I'm greeted by the sight of a large, rustic-looking kitchen. Mouthwatering smells waft over to us from the large ovens coating one of the walls, and several people chatter softly as they bustle around the room like bees.

Kezia turns to me with a bemused expression. "Go on, then."

"Alright, let me see." I hum, tapping my chin as I pretend to think. "A goddess, who willingly lives in the Underworld, and genuinely enjoys wearing corsets..." I click my fingers and point at her. "You're Hecate!"

"Give the girl a gold star, she knows her Greek deities!" Kezia bows sarcastically. "Original Witch and Ruler of the Night, at your service."

I can't help but laugh at her. "So what exactly is it that you do down here? Turn the dead into slugs to entertain yourself?"

"Oh, you know, just the general blood sacrifice every other week. I'm kidding." She laughs at the horrified look on my face. "I help Hades monitor his on-Earth agents most of the time. When I'm really bored, I cook."

"His on-Earth agents?" I gape. "You cook?"

"You'd probably know his agents more commonly as ghosts." She grins when my jaw drops. "Yes, before you ask, ghosts are real. What you mortals don't know, however, is those ghosts are actually just spirits Hades has employed to be his agents on the ground, to keep him up to date with what's happening on Ground Zero. That was my idea, initially; it's why I'm the goddess of ghosts and necromancy. And I mostly like to cook savoury meals, but I do like to experiment with the odd sweet dish. I don't know what it is; I guess I just love cooking with meat."

"There are so many things that I want to unpack in that; I literally don't know where to begin."

Kezia laughs. Winking at me, she puts the plates in a sink and claps her hands. Suddenly the kitchen explodes into life, as if the mere sight of Kezia magically made the quiet workers furiously work themselves into a frenzy.

"I'll tell you what. I'll cook you up something real nice, and we can have a big ol' chat about it all."

I can't help the big grin that spreads across my face at her offer. It's like a splash of fresh water after dealing with Hades and his tepid secrecy for so long. "You're kidding."

"Deadly serious." She smirks at her own joke, wiping her hands on a towel. "What do you want, princess? I'll make you anything."

"Anything?" I ask, and she nods. "Well, in that case, I'd love a big dish of lasagna, with a side of don't ever call me that."

Kezia gives me a sly smile. "As you wish, your highness."

— — —

I end up spending a large portion of my afternoon in the kitchen with Kezia, alternating between talking to her and helping her with the many things she ended up cooking.

She didn't actually say anything about it to me, but I got the feeling that she was secretly grateful for the company. While noisy, her kitchen helpers appeared to be nothing but blank slates in human bodies. I think she was thankful that she had someone around who could actually hold an intelligent conversation.

I was eventually kicked out, though, when I accidentally knocked over the big trifle she'd been slaving over for a couple of hours. I apologised profusely for my clumsiness, but I still think she wished the jam on the floor was my blood; she very nearly knocked me out cold with a punch. Despite the less-than-ideal ending to our afternoon together, though, she promised to come and find me when she had a spare moment; and I was going to hold her to that. Even though Kezia had an incredibly abrasive personality, and, quite frankly, scared me more than I'd like to admit, I got the feeling she'd become one of my closer friends throughout my stay here. She was like a fresh slap to the face, and in the dull environment of the Underworld, I really needed that.

Before I'd royally pissed Kezia off, I'd managed to extract a map of sorts from her regarding the palace layout. So, once she unceremoniously slammed the door in my face, I set out exploring again, determined to find the library. Ironically enough, once I actually had some inkling of where I was going, the palace became ten times easier to navigate, and I ended up finding the library extremely quickly.

The moment I walk through the large mahogany doors, a gasp escapes me, my eyes widening in wonder. The room in front of me is absolutely beautiful. The walls are covered from top to bottom in elegant, arching, wooden bookshelves, full to the brim with books of different sizes, shapes and colours. Ornate crystal chandeliers dangle down from the ceiling, sending golden light skittering around the room like miniature stars. Sitting in front of the crackling, flickering fire is a luscious, forest-green sofa, adorned with an array of intricately embroidered cushions. There's even a rustic wooden ladder leaning delicately against a nearby bookshelf. It looks like a typical, old-style library from a movie, and it takes all my restraint not to squeal like an over-excited fangirl. I can already tell I'm going to spend a lot of my time in here.

Shutting the doors quietly behind me, I hum softly to myself as I let my gaze stream over the books stacked in the shelves. It doesn't take me long to spot some of the classics, like Beowulf or Homer's The Odyssey, but a lot of the titles I don't recognise, and some aren't even in English. After a few minutes, I begin to recognise a trend in the book topics; they're all related to mythology.

I can't help but grin to myself at that. Maybe Hades was more vain than I initially pegged him to be.

After perusing the shelves for a good half hour, I finally decide on a book about Norse mythology and settle myself down on the sofa. I'm right in the process of curling up in front of the fire, determined to read until my brain falls out, when I see something glinting at me from behind two massive bookshelves. Frowning, I place my book down and walk over to inspect the bookshelves. As I draw closer, I notice a small gap between the bookshelves, large enough for me to slip through. So, I suck my stomach in and shimmy through.

I expect to find many things when I finally squeeze my way through — a dungeon, a secret lair, heck, even a shrine — but a hidden music room was definitely not one of them. The darkened room, while as large and grandeur as every other room in the palace, looks like it hasn't been entered in years. The lightswitches collect coats of dust in the corners; half of the instruments lie forgotten under a heavy black cloth; and the majestic, white grand piano that stands centre stage — which I realise is what I'd seen glinting at me from the fireplace — looks sombre and neglected. My curiosity piques. I straighten out my knitted jersey, and cross over to the rest of the covered instruments. I strain for a few seconds as I try to pull the heavy cloth off, but when I finally succeed, my eyes widen in astonishment.

I've never been much of a musician — I was always more interested in the stories hidden between the pages of my books, despite Axel's immense disappointment — but even I knew that the instruments lying in front of me were breathtaking. They were made from the same pure white wood as the piano, and many had golden, sky-blue or grass-green patterns adorning their slim bodies. The refined elegance of them leads me to assume that they had been designed for a girl; exactly who, I wasn't sure. All of a sudden, I feel like an intruder in the abandoned room; like I was staring down at the bare bones of a disregarded past.

Crouching down, I pick up a small violin and investigate it further. The strings were a light silver, like they were spun from starlight itself, and there were intricate gold and blue engravings swirling all around the edges like tangled vines. I study it closer, and realise there's a small name etched into the neck of the violin.

Per—

"Hardly anybody has ever found this room." An inaudible voice says from behind me. I yelp, and whirl around in surprise. Hades watches me from the shadows. It takes all my strength not to throw the violin at him. "How did you?"

"Why do you always creep up on me?!" I shriek, still in shock. He doesn't answer me. "I was curious, okay? Surely you know that about me by now!"

"Curiosity is a dangerous thing." Hades tells me, his midnight-blue eyes flashing. "Most predominantly when you discover things that did not want to be found."

"Where would humanity be if we didn't discover those things, then?" I shoot back. "You're immortal; you must have realised by now that humans are stupidly curious. It's in my nature!"

He regards me for several long seconds, melting out of the shadows. "I frightened you."

"No." I draw the word out sarcastically. "I'm this abrasive normally. Hi, I'm Evie. Nice to freakin' meet you!"

Hades ignores my sarcasm. "It was not my intention to frighten you."

"Shocker." I mutter under my breath, running a shaky hand through my hair. "What is this place, anyway?"

"It is a music room."

"I can see that. Thank you, Captain Obvious." I retort. My fingers unconsciously strum the violin strings. "Why is it hidden away?"

"No reason." He replies. The cold bite to his tone suggests otherwise.

My anger dissipates. I watch him sadly. "You know, at some point you're going to have to trust me too, Hades. Otherwise, my stay here is going to be miserable and boring, for the both of us."

Once again, he doesn't say anything in response. But I'm almost certain I hear him sigh.

I let out a heavy breath, crouching down and placing the violin back down with the rest of its counterparts. I speak softly. "Would you like me to leave?"

"No. That is unnecessary." He speaks just as quietly, his tone impassive. His gaze slowly wanders around the room. "I have not been here for many years. I was under the impression that it had simply disappeared; it is no longer a part of my Elysium. It brings back many unwanted memories."

I straighten. "Of who?"

"Persephone."

My eyes widen rapidly. I speak gingerly, hardly daring to breathe.

"Where is she now?"

"Gone." That one word seems to send a bolt of torment through Hades. And though he tries to hide it, I can see, clear as day, the raw pain it causes him.

Even though a part of me was internally rejoicing that he was finally, finally starting to open up to me, an even bigger part of me was just further confused. Persephone was a goddess, which meant that she couldn't die; so where was she? Sure, I had noticed that she wasn't around — either that or she was really good at hiding — and Hades' admission only fueled my suspicion that she had, for some reason, left. That still left me with one, burning question though.

Where was Persephone?

I shoot Hades a small, reassuring smile. "I'm sorry."

He inclines his head, watching me through hooded eyes. "Did you play?"

"What? Oh, this?" I blink at the abrupt change of subject and point at the violin. He nods. "I used to, when I was eleven. But Axel got sick of me being an all round abhorrent student, so I stopped." I laugh at the memory. "I enjoyed it, though. While it lasted."

"Would you want to learn again?" He asks, surprising me. I stare at him in shock. He raises an eyebrow at me. "I am not a horrible person Evie, much as I am sure you have convinced yourself otherwise. I do enjoy getting to know you."

"I know that you're not a horrible person." My mind travels back two months ago, back to when he'd first brought me here. I'd feared and hated him so much at the beginning. All that shock and anger felt so ridiculous now. "Well, now, anyway. I'm just... surprised that you're asking."

"Why?"

"Because... Well... Based on all our previous encounters, I find it hard to believe that you willingly want to be around me." I try not to sound bitter — emphasis on the 'try'.

Hades sighs lightly, shoving his hands in his trench coat pockets. "No matter how caustic I act Evie, you need to know that that is nobody's fault except my own. I enjoy your company much more than you probably realise."

His comment, as usual, has me desperately wanting to know more; but I know it's as close to an apology as I'll get, so I take it, and answer his question instead.

"In all honesty, I don't think I would enjoy learning again. As much as I'd love to be able to say I can play an instrument, I don't really have the patience to stick with it. Besides, I still have PTSD from when Axel tried to teach me."

My comment elicits a laugh from him. "Why is that?"

I smile, half in embarrassment. "Axel used to threaten to beat me with my violin when I messed up."

"Well, I assure you, I would never do that." Hades tells me, his magnetic blue eyes twinkling. "After all, you will need to walk for the Winter Solstice."

"Winter Solstice?"

"My family holds an annual dance on the eve of the Winter Solstice, every year." Hades explains. "It is their excuse of attempting to force 'family bonding time' on those of us who are less willing to socialise. For you, it will be an opportunity to see the other gods again."

I can see the small hint of a smirk on his lips when he emphasises 'gods', almost like he's poking fun at me.

My stomach drops all the way to China. "The others?"

"Yes," I know he notices the change in my demeanour, but thankfully, he doesn't comment on it. "I know how you feel about them, but—"

"No." I interrupt him, shaking my head and flashing him what I hope is a brave smile. "I'll go. I need to make things right. Besides, you'll be there. What's the worst that could happen?"

What I don't tell him is that a small part of me is secretly looking forward to going.

And the reason I'm looking forward to going?

Him.

www.ingramcontent.com/pod-product-compliance
Lightning Source LLC
Chambersburg PA
CBHW070405200726
48294CB00003B/1092